HOT TO
THE TOUCH

HOT TO THE TOUCH

VIEWS FROM THE
POLYAMORY LIFESTYLE

Edited by
Cole Riley

CLEiS
PRESS

Published in the United States by Cleis Press, an imprint of Start Midnight, LLC, 221 River Street, 9th Floor, Hoboken, NJ 07030.

Printed in the United States.
Cover design: Allyson Fields
Cover photograph: iStock
Text design: Frank Wiedemann
First Edition.
10 9 8 7 6 5 4 3 2 1

Trade ISBN: 978-1-62778-297-5
Ebook ISBN: 978-1-62778-510-5

Contents

vii   *Foreword*

xiii   *Introduction*

1   *Meet My Husband* • JANINE ASHBLESS

15   *Ghost Swinger* • AMANDA EARL

26   *The Dinner Party* • REMITTANCE GIRL

56   *Because of Bingo* • REBECCA M. KYLE

66   *Bob & Carol & Ted (But Not Alice)*
    • M. CHRISTIAN

76   *Homecoming* • TERESA NOELLE ROBERTS

91   *Snakefruit* • ANNE TOURNEY

106   *Him* • SOMMER MARDSEN

113   *Speed Play* • ABIGAIL EKUE

132   *Between Two Lovers* • THOMAS S. ROCHE

150   *Reminder* • JEREMY EDWARDS

163   *Sleeper Car* • MAX LAGOS

169   *The Benefit of the Doubt* • COLE RILEY

179   *One Last Fling* • KRISTINA WRIGHT

201   *About the Authors*

204   *About the Editor*

FOREWORD

Love, relationships, building families, and enjoying a sense of community and belonging are desires that we all seek to fulfill as human beings—part of our shared humanity. Our sense of self-worth, the pursuit of happiness, and in many ways our own survival depends on it.

Growing up in a sex-negative world that spotlights and idealizes heteronormative monogamy, and in some cases "compulsory monogamy," can be challenging because this prescribed framework does not work for everyone. The purpose of this collection, *Hot to the Touch: Views from the Polyamory Lifestyle,* is to create more awareness of alternative lifestyles and forms of love, intimacy, and healthy sexuality.

I was invited to write a foreword for this book partly because of a community I have created, Loving Without Boundaries. At Loving Without Boundaries (LWB), we believe that loving who you want, how you want, in a way that feels natural and comfortable should be a fundamental human right. The name LWB underscores breaking free from the societal norms of monogamy, religion, shame, and guilt to be able to live a life that we create by our own choices. Also, the name stresses that we should be able to explore our own authenticity, love, and connections as we choose. The LWB community is geared toward those practicing consensual non-monogamy of all kinds with an emphasis on polyamory and the poly-curious.

What is polyamory?

Polyamory—the custom or practice of engaging in multiple romantic relationships with the knowledge and consent of all partners concerned.

The term is created by the root *poly* meaning *many* added to the root *amore* meaning *love*. This is in contrast to the word and practice of monogamy, which normally refers to one exclusive romantic and sexual relationship at a time. Many confuse the term *polyamory* with *polygamy*, which denotes multiple marriages at the same time—an act that is illegal in almost all areas of the United States. In contrast, polyamory is a relationship structure that has little to do with the legal bonds of marriage. Most importantly, polyamory and open relationships in general are not just about the sex! Some of the benefits of practicing polyamory are deepened communication skills, major opportunities for personal growth, less pressure to be "all the things" for one partner, an expanded sense of family and support networks, more parental figures and guidance for children, and the ability to create chosen families versus families created traditionally by bloodline or the law.

I'm an advocate for the choice of all human beings to have the option to live traditional or alternative lifestyles if they so choose. I live an alternative lifestyle in that I live a consensually non-monogamous life. I'm a married, polyamorous woman who lives with my two partners: my husband of twelve years and my "beloved" of over three years. I say "beloved" because there is not yet a term that easily identifies my relationship to my other partner. "Boyfriend" sounds too simplistic to me and does not honor the quality and commitment of this relationship and how it feels in my heart. Living a polyamorous lifestyle is an unusual, charming, and an often challenging choice. But for me, it has been less of a choice, and more a statement reflecting who I am inside . . . an orientation.

You see, I'm a former cheating serial monogamist. I came to the polyamorous lifestyle somewhat by accident, but looking back, I was always polyamorous but did not know this relationship structure was available to me. My world, relationships, love, and life have always been constrained by artificial boundaries defined by societal expectations. Those societal boundaries were so strong that I didn't even know that there was a world where consensual non-monogamy and kink openly existed. I grew up attending a Catholic school where I was taught that sex was "dirty" and only for procreation, that masturbation was strictly forbidden, and that homosexuals were deviants and therefore "going to hell." I have spent much of my adult life undoing the damage that was done by this teaching in my formative years. It wasn't until high school and college that I really started to question these teachings.

Today I'm an artist, writer, activist, and unshakable optimist dedicated to creating positive change in the world starting with our own individual freedom to love. As a fellow soul sharing this great planet we are fortunate to inhabit, I believe in each of us pursuing happiness in whatever way we see fit.

So many of us are taught to believe in the scarcity model based on fear surrounding relationships, and thus many relationships are dysfunctional or fail altogether creating unhappiness, disconnection, and isolation. Yet given all the individuals in the world, there simply is not only one type of relationship structure that works for everyone. A romantic relationship is collaboration—a joint creative project to build something as unique and individual as the people creating it. Yet we live in a society where monogamous, heterosexual pairing is how the overwhelming majority of relationships are structured.

We are taught to desire and seek one mate—the one person who will make us whole and happy for the rest of our lives. Then supposedly we will no longer desire others. That's a lot of pressure to be the ideal for each other! Some call this the "romance myth"—the heterosexual, monogamous romance. Since we are socialized in a culture that teaches us that monogamy is right and natural, it is often not a conscious choice for people but more of a default in the creation of relationships.

However, monogamy does not seem to be working well for all as evidenced by the high divorce rates, with roughly one third citing infidelity as the cause. Cheating is rampant in society, with many believing they have no choice.

This is simply not true. We do have choices. We can all choose to conduct our lives using ethics, integrity, and honesty.

We can be proud of who we see in the mirror, increasing self-worth and self-acceptance while reducing depression, shame, and guilt. If monogamy is not working for you, you can choose consensual non-monogamy or polyamory.

The LWB mission helps one see the world in abundance versus scarcity, with a sense of happiness that the world and healthy, loving relationships are within our control. My mission—and the mission of the collection here—is to teach people that they have more choices than they may realize.

Our mission is to help change the way we as society view relationships and connect with each other, as well as how we view ourselves. It is imperative to understand that we are all valuable and deserving of love, even if one is part of a sexual minority. Everyone has the right as well as an innate desire to be loved, to have a sense of belonging, and to conduct their lives as they wish.

My hope is for people to feel that they are free to choose who to love and how to love, free from discrimination and ridicule. Let us all help create a world where there is more tolerance, understanding, and acceptance for unconventional relationships and sexual minorities.

I truly believe that we can improve the quality of our lives by improving the quality of our relationships, one conversation at a time. At the end of each of our life journeys, it is love and the quality of our connections that we will cherish and hold dear to our hearts, no matter which path we choose to get there— monogamous, polyamorous, or otherwise.

We need a revolution of love and hope. We need more relationships of equality and sexual freedom. I invite you to follow your curiosities by enjoying the rest of this important anthology.

Go forth and love,

Kitty Chambliss, ACC, CPC, ELI-MP
National speaker, author, relationship coach, fellow warrior, creator of the Loving Without Boundaries Revolution

INTRODUCTION

This new collection, *Hot to the Touch: Views from the Poly-amory Lifestyle,* is probably the most difficult anthology I've done. The Poly life, an alternative way of love and commitment, is largely underground, which means it's hiding in plain sight. There are clubs, membership meet-and-greets, and closed specialized associations on the Internet, but this lifestyle is growing and thriving.

What is *polyamory*? People may fantasize that the term implies wanton, full-out orgies with all of the rules thrown out the window. Polyamory is not about group sex, swinging, or some complicated erotic fantasy.

Polyamory has been around in some variation for thousands of years. In Islam and some African societies, the male was permitted to have as many as five wives. In Judaism, men of prominence had multiple wives, and the Mormon faith only recently abolished its traditional practice of polygamy. Women have multiple male lovers in the Mosuos in China, as well as parts of Tibet, India, and Sri Lanka.

In today's Western world, typically two people fall in love and marry for life. Possibly because of the high divorce rate, the door has been opening for polyamory as an alternative lifestyle. Those who are members of the Poly life consider themselves to be cultural pioneers, social innovators, and outsiders in this conventional buttoned-down society. They suspect the loneliness, deceit, isolation, and boredom that can be a part of conventional monogamy.

Polyamory involves changing the rules of society. The Poly life involves entertaining multiple sexual relationships with the knowledge and consent of all of the partners involved. Stepping out of the traditional comfort zone, lovers and partners can enjoy a variety of Poly activities: open relationships permitting casual and recreational sex with many partners, closed polyamorous coupling with two or more partners, or a single Poly lover out of the group dating a partner with the others' consent.

According to Poly rules, safe sex has to be practiced at all times. Often, the members of the group will go over what sexual practices are acceptable on dates to ensure that no sexual boundaries are crossed. In a recent *Rolling Stone* article, it was estimated that four to five percent of Americans practice polyamory or some type of open relationship. Nearly twenty percent of the population have tried ethical non-monogamy.

This collection, *Hot to the Touch*, puts readers into the heads, hearts, and libidos of lovers and partners exploring the Poly lifestyle or something that resembles the risk and boldness of unconventional intimacy. Some of them enjoy the provocative existence, while others do not have a label for what they feel.

The Poly life demands that all partners be emotionally and sexually satisfied. A classic story by Sommer Madsen finds another woman taking on many lovers to suit her man's desires, because nothing is too good for "Him." In old school affairs of the heart, most of the parties are only concerned with themselves, but not in these unorthodox relationships.

One of the jewels of the collection, "Bob & Carol & Ted (But Not Alice)," penned by veteran wordsmith M. Christian, does not include the lovely Natalie Wood or perky Dyan Cannon. In this gonzo tale of multiple lovers on the make, the characters are determined to get their share of erotic fun and frolic. Jeremy Edwards, well-known erotica scribe, depicts the ultimate lust of sensual temptation in his fanciful "Reminder." In what is the possible stunner of the collection, Anne Tourney's memorable "Snakefruit," reveals a snapshot of a sexually pent-up pregnant woman, experiencing a lull in her marital sex life, wooed by her hubby's rebellious brother-in-law.

At the heart of the book celebrating some of the essential themes of the Poly lifestyle are: Janine Ashbless's "Meet My Husband," Teresa Noelle Roberts's "Homecoming," Rebecca M. Kyle's "Because of Bingo," Kristina Wright's "One Last Fling," Amanda Earl's "Ghost Swinger," my own "The Benefit of the Doubt," and Remittance Girl's exotic "The Dinner Party."

Hot to the Touch: Views from the Polyamory Lifestyle explores many notions of love, desire, dating, commitment, sexual secrets, betrayal, fantasy, and obsession. These stories seek to uncover new ground as they search out sex and love under the banners of polyamory and monogamy. They challenge us to dream, imagine, and think. Enjoy these outrageous, sensual adventures about those who enjoy the Poly lifestyle or are just poly-curious.

Cole Riley
New York City

MEET MY HUSBAND

Janine Ashbless

"What do you think of him?" Cassie asked. The opportunity had presented itself while she was spooning homemade tiramisu onto dessert plates and Andrew was loading the dishwater with the crockery he'd brought in from the back of the house. Jeff was still outside on the lawn, beer in hand, enjoying the garden view over the dying embers of the barbeque.

Andrew hesitated. "He's not . . . like I'd imagined him, from what you'd said."

"What do you mean?" Cassie couldn't remember how she'd described the other man. She'd actually done her best not to talk much about Jeff to Andrew, or vice-versa. It would, she felt, be impolite to gossip—a breach of confidence—and she wasn't a teenager, compelled to blab her relationships to all and sundry. It was much more adult to keep those two spheres, boyfriend and husband, separate.

Until now, anyway.

"You said he was a landscaper. Heavy lifting, son of the soil, all that. But he's sharp. He knows his economics." There'd been a discussion about mortgages and banking.

"Don't be such a snob," she laughed.

"He's older than your last boyfriends too."

"A bit. Does it bother you that he's not just a slab of man-meat?"

Andrew looked grave. "Does he like opera?"

"Absolutely hates it."

"Then I'm probably safe," he concluded, dryly, so that she laughed and threw her arms round his neck. *He's so cute*, she thought.

"Take out one of the plates and the cream," she told him after their lingering kiss.

They emerged from the back door together to find Jeff examining the cascades of purple flowers that grew in profusion all over their cast-iron Victorian veranda. "Nice wisteria," he said. "Sorry . . . busman's holiday."

The sight of his lean khaki-clad body and his craggy face made Cassie's heart sing, and she was bemused that he had this effect on her. Constantly. "It's lovely at this time of year," she said, laying out dessert on the lawn table. "Nearly as old as the house, I think."

They ate, talking idly about the garden. Jeff stretched his long legs out on a stool. Cassie could feel the light tension between the three of them, like the faintest tug of a thread. This was the first time the two men had met, the first time she'd introduced any of her boyfriends to her husband. Jeff was different. It had been nearly a year, for starters. And it was, with him, more than just sex. They had interests in common. They ran mini-triathlons and half-marathons together. And they went out in public, as a couple, to gigs that Andrew would rather cut his ears off than attend.

"It's a bit weird, this," Jeff said with a quiet smile. "Not what I pictured." It was as if he'd turned a key. The one central topic of conversation was unlocked.

"How's that?" Andrew asked, pulling another beer from the icebox and passing the open bottle over to him. Andrew wasn't even slightly nervous, not like her. Andrew was famously unflappable.

"I don't know." Jeff looked briefly skyward, a signal of self-effacement. "From what Cass said, I just pictured someone more . . . monkish."

What I said? I don't seem to have given anyone *the right impression!*

Andrew grinned. "What did she tell you?"

Jeff gestured vaguely with his bottle. "You know. The whole . . . academic thing?"

Cassie covered her mouth, trying not to smirk. Andrew was a lecturer, and he had a bit of a dad-bod, and he didn't run—but he lifted weights every night and had an inclination toward being barrel-chested, so despite the natural tonsure (which was offset by his beard anyway), no, he didn't look monkish at all.

But that wasn't really what Jeff had meant, was it? And Andrew knew that.

"We have sex a couple of times a week," he said, "if that's what you're asking. It might not to be up to your personal standards—but statistically speaking, that's pretty good for a couple of our age."

Yes. Lovely, cuddly, comfortable sex. She smiled at her husband and put a hand on his thigh, feeling a surge of love for him.

Jeff cleared his throat, his eyes flicking back and forth between them. He was on Andrew's home territory, after all.

"Look, I'm going to be straight here. She adores you. She still fucks you. You've got this . . ." He gestured around at the garden, the house, the sunny afternoon. "This great life together. I've got to wonder: what am I bringing to the table?"

"Andrew doesn't run," Cassie said. "And he doesn't go see Whitesnake."

"And," said Andrew, "I don't do kink."

Jeff looked at him dubiously down the neck of his bottle, which made Cassie giggle.

"I don't spank," her husband said. "Pain squicks me out. I can't fake dominance. Sorry, just not my thing. Poor Cassie finds it very frustrating. Not a kinky bone in my body."

"Oh—not exactly true," Cassie said, poking him in the leg with one finger.

Jeff's puzzled frown met his amused smile at the level of his eyes, crinkling the skin. "Yeah?"

"He likes to watch," Cassie said.

Andrew spread his hands in a gesture of acquiescence. "Well. I'm a lecturer in fine arts," he excused himself.

"His girlfriend's a nude life-model. And a pole dancer. She likes to flash it about, and Andrew loves to go watch her showing off."

Jeff pointed a finger. "Wait. You've got a girlfriend too?"

"Didn't Cassie tell you?"

"Uh-uh. Is she, uh . . . with you too, Cass?"

"No." This wasn't a lie, though she felt her cheeks warm. Cassie didn't lie to her lovers. Spanking didn't count as sex, she had decided. It wasn't as if she was into other women—she just enjoyed paddling Kayleigh's pretty ass. It wasn't sex if she never even got her hands dirty, was it?

"And you're okay with that?"

"I like her," Cassie said. "She's a nice kid. She likes to go to horrible modern art exhibitions with Andy while not wearing anything under her skirt."

"Kid?"

She rolled her eyes. "Kayleigh's twenty-eight . . . and a single mother. Sorry, at my age almost everyone seems young. Even you."

"There's only seven years difference," he reminded her. "And you're not old yet." He winked. "I've seen you naked, remember?"

She blew him a kiss for his gallantry.

"How did you two hit it off?" Andrew wondered. Cassie waited for Jeff's version.

"Uh . . . We were at a Sunday park run. I'd only started a few months beforehand, so I was very much part of the main herd. The thing I've found is, if you can spot a fine ass and try to keep it in sight, it somehow makes things a *lot* easier. I saw this fine round little pair of cheeks come twinkling past me and I just thought, *I'm following this.* So I did—all the way to the finish line. Hypnotized, I was. My best time to date by miles. Then I said hi."

"And did I want to go out for a late breakfast?" Cassie added.

"And that was when she said she was married, over scrambled egg on toast. But that it was all right. Because she was allowed. Which seemed just really weird to me."

"But you fucked her anyway," Andrew noted with an amused twinkle. Cassie felt her blush deepen.

"Yeah." Jeff smiled fondly at the memory. "I took her back to my place and ate out her beautiful pussy and fucked it *very* thoroughly. Then I pounded that peachy ass . . . until she screamed so loud the old dear upstairs banged on the ceiling in protest."

The warm air suddenly seemed harder to breathe. Cassie was aware of the heave of her breasts as she inhaled.

"Talking of neighbors . . ." said Andrew thoughtfully, and indicated the hedge with a sideways glance. "Should we perhaps continue this conversation indoors?"

Jeff nodded.

Cassie abandoned her dessert plate but took her wineglass. She felt giddy, but she doubted it was the fault of the single glass of chilled chardonnay.

"Want a top-up on that?" Andrew asked, and she nodded. As he scooted away to the kitchen Jeff intercepted her under the veranda, blocking her path through the cane furniture.

"Did I hear you right—you're not into Andrew's peek-a-boo fantasies?"

She shook her head. "I like to keep my private parts *private*."

"So you've never done it in the garden?"

"No." Her inner alarms were aquiver now; she knew that husky, considering tone in Jeff's voice. She knew where those roving glances were headed.

"Not even in the hot tub?"

She flushed. They'd fooled around a bit. But she really didn't like the idea of the neighbors judging her. "No."

"Or under here?" He indicated the structure of the veranda, its open walls almost sealed off by the heavy droops of leaves and flowers, the sunlight and shadows flickering where the breeze tried to break through. It made a lambent green room, humid with the smell of growing life.

"Nope."

"Oh well," he said with a grin. "Baby steps." He looked down at her summer dress, blue cotton with a pink-rose print, and put a fingertip lightly on the not-quite-risqué, almost-intimate skin of her breastbone. "Now take those panties down."

"Jeff . . ." she chided.

"What? You scared your husband might suspect something's

going on between us?" His finger traced a path downward and the voice behind his grin was low, and warm, and teasing. But there was an edge of iron in there that made her knees go weak. "I've got a kiss for you, but you need to earn it. Take them off, now."

Andrew hadn't come back into view. Cassie took a deep breath and pulled her panties down and off. She wanted that kiss, after all—she'd been two hours in his company with hardly a touch, and she wasn't used to that. She yearned to feel Jeff's mouth on hers.

He held his hand out and she dropped the claret-colored thong with the lace sides into his open palm. Jeff rubbed it between his fingers. "Wet," he said, tucking it into the breast pocket of his shirt. "Who's secretly been getting all worked up, you bad girl?"

Of course she'd been getting worked up. She'd been sitting with her husband and her lover, watching both, enjoying the contrasts, yearning to break out of their stultifying politeness and touch *somebody*. She cast him a *you-got-me* look.

Then Jeff pulled her slowly toward him and she lifted her arms about his neck, stretching up on her toes. She slid into his kiss like it was a hot bath that lapped every inch of her shivering skin. So rapt was she in the tug and tease of his mouth that it took her a moment too long to register the movement of his hands inside the spaghetti straps of her dress and down her back, deftly unclipping her matching bandeau bra. As he released her he pulled it off completely, leaving her naked beneath the thin cotton dress.

Cassie flashed a protest with her eyes, but he wasn't looking that high. His free hand covered her right breast, shaping the material against its soft orb and stiff nipple. His mouth tugged in a smile even as his fingertips tugged at her, making her exhale a long whimper.

"Bad, bad girl," he breathed, and she felt the heat and the weight of her desire swell between her thighs. "You'd better sit down nicely before your husband notices what a state you're in." He dropped his hand, accurately, to the juncture of her legs and stroked her mons through the dress with his fingertips. That light touch was enough to stagger her.

That was the moment that Andrew walked back onto the veranda, a wineglass and two frosted bottles of beer in hand. He stopped in mid-stride, taking in the scene before him. For a wild, vain moment Cassie hoped that he wouldn't spot that she was bra-free, that Jeff would somehow palm the garment or drop it discretely behind a piece of furniture. But Andrew couldn't help noticing, and no wonder—the soft and clinging dress fabric was tented now over the twin points of her nipples, which stood despite the day's warmth as stiff and proud as they ever had; like blunted sticks of artists' chalk.

"That's a good look," he said sagely. "I can see that you've been keeping our guest entertained, Cassie."

Jeff slung the red bra over his shoulder.

Blushing furiously, she reached for her glass. But Andrew turned his back, taking the drinks over to an occasional table next to a wicker armchair and setting them down carefully on the glass surface. "Don't let me interrupt you two. You won't mind if I watch, will you?"

She swayed, her body a battleground of conflicting emotions. Damn it, why did they insist on mixing things up? She liked to keep her men in separate boxes in her head.

But maybe men didn't belong in boxes, she told herself.

"Sit down, Cass," ordered Jeff. The nearest chair was a wicker stool with a foam cushion. She took a step over, and was about to plop herself down when he added, "Facing Andrew."

Light-headed, she obeyed, perching on the edge of the cushion with her spine ramrod straight from nerves, even though she knew that it pushed her bust out into higher, jutting relief. Her fingers were tangled together in her lap. She felt grateful for the press of the cushion between her splayed thighs, against her sex—it seemed to anchor her.

Andrew, his expression unreadable, settled himself into the armchair as if in a theater.

"Are you embarrassed, Cass?" Jeff asked. "Letting your husband see you in this state?"

It *was* embarrassing, which was crazy. They'd been married for two decades, after all. They knew each other inside and out. There was no mystery and no excitement. Their relationship was respectful, kindly, and trusting—everything you'd want from your husband and the father of your grown children.

Well, almost everything.

She bit her lip and nodded. Andrew's gaze was glued to the unfettered quiver of her breasts, which made her feel strange. Shouldn't familiarity breed contempt? He'd seen them every day, and watched her nurse two kids with those. Jeff's lust was something she believed in, gleefully, but it was hard to imagine that after all this time her husband could feel any genuinely dirty, *disturbing* lust for her.

"Now pull your dress down and let him see you playing with your nipples," said Jeff.

Her hands tried to obey. But her own gaze jumped around, from Andrew's face then out sideways at the sunlit garden beyond the wisteria, and she hesitated. The familiar scenery balked her. *Why is this so hard? Why do I stand on my dignity with Andrew but not Jeff?* Her husband was used to the sensible Cassie. The pragmatic, rational Cassie that he'd relied on for twenty-plus years.

She didn't want him to see her other side. That undignified, unthinking submissive. The fool for love.

Jeff's snort was either exasperated or amused, she couldn't tell. "Stop looking out there," he said softly, and she glimpsed him at the edges of her vision, wielding the wireless bandeau. "Pay attention." Slipping it over her eyes as a blindfold he tied it at the back of her head. For a moment she felt panic, and then just as suddenly realized that it was reassuring, in the strangest way. Her world, plunged into scarlet darkness, suddenly narrowed down to the thud of her pulse and the weight of Jeff's hands on her shoulders from behind. She reached out a little farther with her senses, smelling the sweet flowers of the climbing plant over-head, hearing the creak of the wicker under Andrew's weight as he shifted in his seat. But she couldn't sense anything beyond that; not the garden or the house or any watchful, prurient neighbors.

"They might hear," she whispered.

"Then you'll have to keep really, really quiet."

She could feel Jeff's warm, slightly leathery hands—cupping only her shoulders but somehow laying claim to her whole body, their weight slight but somehow pinning her in place at the center of a spinning world.

"Lift up your skirt," he told her.

She found that she could, this time. It was easier without having to see anyone watching. An inch at a time she drew the cotton skirt up her thighs, and to reward her obedience Jeff's hands slipped down to play with her breasts, baring them. When he caught her nipples she gasped and sighed, sensation flooding across her skin in quicksilver ripples.

"Now open your legs."

She stared wide-eyed into the claret-hued blur. It was like the glowing red blind in Jeff's bedroom window when they fucked together on sunlit afternoons. It was like the red space in her head when his cock slid up her ass and orgasm overtook her. She clung to that vision, not letting any image of Andrew intrude, but letting Jeff's instruction wash through her, down from the tingling nape of her neck through her aching breasts to her arched feet.

Slowly she opened her thighs, running her fingertips from the rucked folds of her skirt across the bare and silky skin below. She wasn't sure how much Andrew could see, or what he was doing.

"Good girl," Jeff said, tugging the points of her breasts with precise and delicious cruelty. "Now stand up and bend over the chair. Give him a view of your bottom."

She forced her unsteady legs beneath her, turning to lean over the cushion, which squished beneath her braced palms. Jeff pulled her skirt up from above, so that the hemline hovered almost—but not quite—at a level that shielded her modesty.

"What I have appreciated," Andrew commented in a dreamy voice, "is the way you've got her to go shaven since she started seeing you. *L'Origine du Monde* aside, it's very much the artists' aesthetic, after all."

Cassie felt a blushing giggle escape. She'd felt guiltily frivolous every time she stripped her pussy. *Mutton dressed as lamb*, she'd told her reflection in the mirror. But it seemed that both her men thought differently. It gave her the courage to spread her ankles wider, feeling the breeze tickle her intimately.

There was a jingle of belt buckle, a rasp of tiny metal teeth. *Oh my—*

"Mouth open, Cass," said Jeff, pressing up against her, a sensory confusion of cotton and zipper and hot, hard flesh against her face and lips. Though he was so erect that she had to work at taking it all, it was an act of pure and joyous instinct to yield to his cock's insistence. "Ah, there you go. Yes. All the way."

"May I?" Cassie heard from behind her.

"Go for it," said Jeff.

Go for what? She couldn't see anything, and she didn't know what Andrew was planning. Was he going to touch her wet, unguarded pussy? She'd like that, she realized. She wanted to be touched back there while Jeff's cock slipped in and out of her throat.

But "Umph," was all she could grunt around his length, so she jiggled her ass hopefully, arching her back to drop a broader hint. Andrew cleared his throat, almost a grunt—but he didn't touch her. Not with hand or cock. Jeff's thrusts became deeper and slower, staking a claim to her entire attention. Part of her wanted him to come like that, to feel him spurt and fill and choke her.

But not her pussy. Her pussy wanted attention.

Shifting her torso's weight to one arm, she reached down between her legs with the other hand, comforting her swollen clit.

Jeff rocked to a pause. "Thirsty, girl?" he asked, pulling her mouth all the way off his length, root to glans, so that she trailed spit. "Up." As she straightened he shifted forward, pulling off her dress and straddling the stool as he threw the garment aside. She heard it creak under his bulk as he settled himself. Then without asking for her cooperation he lifted her bodily—in that way that always excited her, like she was a doll, like he could do anything to her he wanted—wrapped her thighs about his hips and pulled her down onto him, impaling her on his erect cock.

That was what her pussy wanted, and Cassie gasped with gratitude as his thick heat filled her emptiness. She didn't even have to rise and fall on him because he did all the work, grasping her splayed asscheeks in his big hands and pulling them wide as he hefted her in short, stuttering jerks. She gripped his neck and rotated her hips and keened deep in her throat as she felt her orgasm build. Sweaty skin slipped beneath her fingers. His fingers dug into her, threatening the clench of her ass.

"Yes!" she squealed, forgetting her fear of being overheard, forgetting to worry about whatever it was her husband was doing or thinking. "Fuck me! Fuck me!"

Jeff sank a finger into her ass and that was enough, it turned out. Cassie came, sharp and long, and then realized that he was rigid beneath her and shooting his load too.

For a long moment they clung together precariously on the stool, and then Jeff laughed, like he did so often after sex—a deep rumble of incredulous pleasure—and kissed her as he pulled off the blindfold. She blinked in the light.

"Up you get, love," Jeff said. She sank onto her knees on the tiles as he eased himself out from beneath her and stood. His shirt was soaked with sweat, and after a moment he pulled it off over his head and mopped at his gleaming chest. "Jesus," he grinned. "I'm hot."

She didn't bother with the obvious joke, but she smirked.

"I'll let you two . . ." he muttered, then took off in a slightly unsteady amble out into the garden, his fat cock still lolling out of his open pants. She watched him go without protest.

Oh, screw the neighbors. If they're peeking through the hedge they deserve everything they get.

She flopped forward on her elbows over the stool, covering her eyes with her hands. It seemed safer blind. "Andy?" she asked. She hadn't heard anything from him. "You okay?"

"Shush, love." The epithet was different when he said it; he didn't call clients and old ladies "love." Just her, and Kayleigh. His hand descended on the small of her back, massaging her, and she stretched with pleasure, the last orgasmic ripples trickling through her and evoking a little moan of delight. Only when he leaned in and kissed her shoulder, though, did she dare look him in the face.

"That was wonderful," he said. His eyes were bright. "That was hands-down the hottest thing I've ever seen."

"You didn't . . ." Had he been stroking off as he watched his wife get fucked by her boyfriend? ". . . come?"

"Not yet. But I will." He put his smartphone down on the cushion between her hands and pressed PLAY. She watched the footage. Saw her spread thighs and her raised ass, and the glistening pink split of her sex below the hem of her skirt. Saw her manicured nail playing with her engorged clit. Saw, in extreme close-up, Jeff's cock plunging up into her stretched pussy, over and over, while his big dark fingers sought out the tight whorl of her ass and penetrated her to make her buck and scream. Saw her boyfriend's pale semen ooze from her sex and hang in viscous drips, then drop and pool on the veranda tiles.

She caught her breath. Andrew's cock tented his still-zipped pants.

"I'm going to enjoy that over and over," he told her. "My beautiful, beautiful wife."

I'm not going to be able to keep them separate now, she thought. *Not ever again.*

GHOST SWINGER

Amanda Earl

D id you know Betty and Bruce are swingers? Course that's not what we called it in our day, is it, Mattie? Back then it was "wife swapping." Oh, I know I wasn't legally your wife at that time. It's not like we were traditionalists. But you swapped me a number of times as I recall, and I swapped you too. We did some swinging as well. Back and forth from lover to lover. Oh, those were glorious times, weren't they, Mattie?

Remember that place? Tofino? That's where we landed our sorry American butts so you could avoid the Vietnam Conflict as our dumb-ass government called it.

Tofino . . . what a wild and rugged landscape it was, right out of a painting. You couldn't call it calm though, could you? And it wasn't just those high winds and big waves, as glorious as they were. We'd watch the waves come rolling off the sea during storms. Wouldn't even wear raincoats, just let the water wash over us both while we watched the light play over the ocean, our own symphony.

But the main reason it wasn't calm was because the whole place was shimmering with unbridled sex. "Free love" we called it. We sure were rebels back then, weren't we, Mattie? Can't imagine how we'd fit in with this rule-abiding bunch.

I've watched them, these swingers. They go to these clubs where you have to be a member to get in. There are different rooms depending on whether you're a voyeur or an exhibitionist, or you want to have casual sex or chat first. It's all so complicated.

Betty seems very partial to some girl her age named Marjorie, and I can't blame her. I bet you'd give young Marjorie a run for her money, wouldn't you, Mattie? Just because we're not twenty anymore doesn't mean we can't dream now and again, does it?

They seem so organized now. You have to make reservations in advance. Some places don't let single guys in. Imagine that. And nobody's allowed to smoke. Yep, not even reefers. You have to show your membership card. Hell, we burnt up cards, didn't we, Mattie? Remember your draft card? We doused it in Jack Daniels and set the fucker on fire.

Ah the world's become so regimented, hasn't it, Mattie? Remember how we'd spread blankets out on top of Radar Hill, eat a few shrooms, and lie under the stars; David on his bongos while the lot of us fucked our brains out under a full moon? We didn't ask for a rule book then, did we? We just danced with somebody, and if they were hip to it, pulled them down onto a blanket.

At the end of the night, I'd wake up and crawl back into our tent, where I'd find you snoring away, some girlie nestled in the crook of your arm. I'd join you and go back to sleep. I still remember how you moaned in surprise when you woke up to not just me but also the other girl sucking your cock and playing with your balls as the rain fell heavy on the roof of the tent. By the time we were done, all sticky with sweat and cum, the only thing to do was to throw our exhausted bodies into the ocean, wash it all off, and start over.

Some guy played guitar as good as Hendrix. Remember him, Mattie? Can't recall his name, but I sure remember his cock and those fine licks he played on his Stratocaster. Nothing like hearing "Red House" as the sun is setting and being sprawled out on the long grass getting my cunt eaten out by a girl who's an expert.

And how lucky was it that the guitar guy ended up being this chick's boyfriend. We all made beautiful music together. Brenda, that was her name, remember? Long black locks that kept getting tangled, sea-green eyes. She looked like a witch or a gypsy. And the guy . . . oh yeah, I remember now, he went by the name of Raven. He had this wild Afro and such gorgeous coffee-colored skin. I was as white as a piece of paper when I got to Tofino, but by the time I'd spent a week making love out in the open under the big Tofino sky, I was bronze and sun kissed. And kissed by a lot of lovers too.

Remember how we partied with Raven and Brenda? Oh, what times we had. Raven introduced us to acid. I still remember how your eyes got all wide, and you wrote the craziest rhymes, all about being in harmony with the universe. The sea looked to us like it was all the colors of a rainbow. You couldn't resist it, said it was luring you in with its colors and beautiful song.

I was a bit worried when you and Brenda, both high as kites, jumped into the waves and pressed your bodies together while Raven and I watched from the shore. But it was such a turn-on seeing the way Brenda dazzled you, watching her seduce you with those sparkling eyes. It was like the two of you became one with the sea. You dragged her with you far out into the ocean and then you both rolled back on the crest of a high wave, sputtering and laughing.

You looked over at me then, and I could see you were a little scared. Maybe the water grabbed at you a bit too forcefully, tried to pull you down. I smiled at you. I wanted to tell you that life was worth living to the full. The only thing to do was grab back at it and fuck the living daylights out of it.

Maybe you read my mind. I wasn't surprised when you pushed Brenda down onto the sand and entered her, and I laughed when the two of you howled as you fucked. Raven and I couldn't resist. We rolled over to where you were and joined in. I lay beside Brenda and parted my legs, looking over at you and laughing. You reached over and touched my naked breasts, making my nipples harden. Raven and you made jokes about our tits, saying we should have a contest to see whose nipples could get hardest.

Both Brenda and I stuck out our tongues and kissed each other while the two of you stroked yourself and watched us. I watched both of you standing in the sand, your cocks hard as rocks as you looked down on us. It turned me on even more.

I took one of Brenda's nipples between my fingers. I seem to remember telling you that the better contest would be to see who could make Brenda's nipples hard. I leaned down and sucked and sucked, tasting the salt from the ocean, then reached over to the other one and tugged on it.

Her nipples glistened with the wetness from my mouth and the water. Her eyes shone as my hand reached down and caressed her beautiful stomach, all golden from the sun. I brushed the kelp from her body. Her hair lay splayed out in the sand, and she was as seductive as a mermaid. I let my hand rove farther and then tickled her inner thighs with the gentle motion of my fingers against her skin. She spread her legs for me. I moved lower until my face was hovering over her cunt like a hummingbird over a flower. I gently parted her lower lips and began licking at the top until I reached her tiny clit. I sucked it into my mouth and Brenda moaned. I placed my finger inside Brenda's warm, welcoming cunt. She moved against it, begging for more. I put another finger in and another, and she cried out. I looked up at you and Raven, and you were rubbing your cocks hard at this point, the sight of me fucking Brenda driving you wild.

The waves were coming in faster now. The tide was going to come in soon. I moved my fingers in and out of Brenda's cunt. She writhed her hips to take them deeper inside. The two of you knelt down to get a closer look. I felt a warm hand on my back.

It was Raven. You and he couldn't let us have all the fun. You moved up to kiss Brenda and Raven slid his fingers along the curve of my back and down to my ass. You straddled Brenda and she took your cock into her mouth while Raven slid his fingers between my asscheeks. I opened for him while I spread Brenda's lower lips wide and slid my tongue inside her cunt, tasting her sweetness. I pressed my lips against her mound and curled my fingers inside her.

Her cries were muffled by your cock stuffed inside her mouth. You used your hand to guide your cock deeper down her throat. Raven danced a finger gently around the rim of my asshole. I wanted him to put it in there. I heard you telling him to stick his finger up my ass. You knew how much I loved ass play, how much I liked to be fucked in that tight, small hole.

Raven moved his finger in and out of me for a while. The beach was completely empty, one of those secluded spots so common in those days, but I doubt we would have cared if others were around. We would have just invited them to join us.

I could feel Raven's cool breath on my back as he leaned over me. He removed his finger and gave me a light slap on the ass. I remember hearing you laughing and thinking I would get you for that later. You knew I liked a little slap now and again, even sometimes a bit rougher, but that was something we hadn't shared with anyone else so far. I looked up at you and frowned, but you just winked and shrugged as if to remind me that anything was possible and that I should just go with the flow. I let my mouth return to Brenda's cunt and licked up all the juices flowing out of her. I changed my hand position so I could maneuver better. Then I pressed my thumb against her asshole and she moaned.

Behind me I felt the pressure of Raven's balls on my ass. I relaxed, waiting for him to enter me. I felt his cock nudge my asshole and then slowly, slowly slide in, waiting for me to relax enough so he could go deeper. I cried out then, told him to fuck me deep.

We were all moving in unison: I was licking Brenda's cunt; you were driving your cock in and out of Brenda's mouth, sometimes rubbing it over her eyes, her nose, and her mouth, letting the precum drip onto her face; Raven's cock was plunging in and out of my ass. It felt like we were all one with each other, with the universe. My asshole tingled with the fullness of Raven's cock, so hard and full of cum inside me. I moved my hips to pull his cock deep inside my ass. It felt so good, so tight. The pressure built. I ground my body into the sand, humping against it and moaning against Brenda's cunt. She screamed as she came, and then I joined her. Soon after I felt splashes of your cum on my neck. Raven kept pumping and pumping into me until he came hard inside my ass. The waves rolled in and soaked us, making us all break apart and sputter with laughter.

We had such a variety of lovers, didn't we? I wonder what happened to Raven and Brenda. I wonder if they stayed together like you and I did. Most of our friends got divorced long ago, but for you and me, it was till death do us part and even then, being with others made it that much better, I think. It made us honest with each other, and it made us coconspirators in a way, sharing our stories, our lovers.

It's not like we were looking for love with any of these people. We just wanted to have fun, to enjoy the moment of bodies merging together.

There's Betty and Bruce now, back from their adventuring. They're on cloud nine. I guess they had fun at the swingers' club. You remember these two don't you, Mattie? She worked summers at my office to earn money for college. We never saw him all that much. There was that one time we all ended up at the same play though, and it was canceled.

Remember that dinner we had? Lots of wine. Us old folks telling them about the goings on back when we were their age. "Flower children" we were called. We told them about our arrival in Tofino, how we ran to the edge of the cliff and gathered up flowers: indian paintbrush, yellow monkey flowers, ferns, and rolled in them together, feeling so young and free and lucky to be alive in that beautiful paradise.

They snickered at that. All sleek and slim they were, wearing black, both of them. Trying to look sophisticated, I guess. They seemed happy though, smiling like the cat that ate the canary. And you seemed quite taken with Betty, if I recall. Of course they didn't admit anything to us about their own adventures; although I sense they wanted to tell us something, they just were a bit shy, I guess. Now we know their secret. About once a month, they get a babysitter for their young toddler, go off and get themselves good and screwed at that swingers' club.

I'm such a voyeur. I couldn't help peeking in on one of their visits to the club, just in time to see Betty kneeling in front of some silver-haired old gent, his cock down her throat. What a heartening thing to see. And that girl knew a trick or two. I got real close. At one point the old fellow asked her if she felt a draft, well that was me, lying on the floor, getting a close-up view of the action. You'd have loved seeing how tenderly and languidly she licked at his balls. You always complained to me how bad some women were at giving head. Never spent enough time on your balls, you said. Betty has some definite possibilities, my dear.

Anyway, Betty gave that old codger a fine blow job. She licked the rim over and over, then slipped the head just a little into her mouth and let the wetness from her mouth run down his cock. When it was all nice and slick, she encircled the shaft and slid his cock in and out of her mouth, giving the old man a combination of hand and mouth. The guy had amazing stamina too and a cock very much like yours, very wide. I'm sure her mouth was tired but she was a real trooper, kept licking, sucking, stroking until he grunted out that he was about to cum. Then the master stroke, she lifted her lithe young body and pressed her tits against his cock, rubbing and rubbing until he exploded all over her chest and cheeks. You could tell she was really turned on. I left at that point, but I wonder if the old guy is as good at tongue-fucking as you are, my love. I doubt it. I wish Betty could experience your talented tongue on her clit.

Bruce was nowhere to be seen. Maybe Betty went home and told him all about her adventures while he jacked off for her. Remember how it was for us, Mattie? How we'd fuck like banshees after we were with other lovers? You only had to see me on my hands and knees, taking another man's cock from behind and you went wild with lust. Said it was the most intimate thing, to be able to watch me with another lover.

Did I ever tell you how moved I was when you sat down beside me as I was straddling that guy, James? You reached up to my face and brushed the hair out of my eyes, touched my back, smiled, and then headed over to your own little party at the other end of the beach. All the time James was fucking me, I felt that hand of yours, beautiful, warming my back. Maybe it's like that for Betty and Bruce.

I see you've got a bulge there, Mattie. Must be getting horny, listening to all these reminiscences. Or maybe it's the thought of Betty and Marjorie lying together at that club. Wonder if Betty and Bruce play games like we did? Maybe they like the sandwich game where the girls are standing up with their tits touching while the men fuck them from behind. Remember how we all tried to walk and ended up falling down? It's a wonder we didn't injure ourselves, isn't it, Mattie? Ah, but we had such fun.

You were so damn fine in your twenties, Mattie. I still remember all the Canadian girls going wild over those sky-blue eyes and that long blond hair of yours when we got off the bus from Seattle.

I guess it was brave of us to plan to set up our lives together in a different country, but we'd heard good things about British Columbia. I remember our long discussions together about Vancouver, where we initially thought we'd go. Lots of guys avoiding the draft ended up in Vancouver. You had contacts there. But remember how we got to talking to that young couple on the bus? They described this place, far out west on the coast in Clayquot Sound. Even the name Clayquot was exotic to us.

I still remember how happy we were to hear that people lived near the beach rent free. They were squatters. We were so broke. Tofino sounded like the perfect place for us. Gosh, how your dad yelled at you when you told him you wouldn't go to war. My parents weren't any better. They wanted me to stop seeing you. I don't know if I ever told you that my father called you a Benedict Arnold; said you were betraying your country.

Of course, we didn't see it that way. And you still don't. I've seen you getting all upset over this Afghanistan thing, rattling the newspaper. Not much changes in this world, eh Mattie? There will always be people fighting but luckily there will also always be people loving, and that's us. By the looks of things, that's Bruce and Betty too.

I wanted to tell you about these two for a reason, Mattie. I think it's time for you to make friends now. I've been gone such a long time, honey. And they're wild like we were, Mattie. I think you'd enjoy their company. And you could tell them about us, about all our escapades, about our lovers and all the different ways we fucked. All the different places. I'm sure they'd love it. I don't want you to be alone. It's time to stop coming here, Mattie. Time you took up your life again.

Once a month Matthew MacGregor visited his wife Alexa's grave, overlooking Radar Hill near Tofino. This time on a crisp autumn late afternoon he brought his friends, Bruce and Betty with him. They drank shots of Jack Daniels beneath the cypress and cedars and watched the sun set while he regaled them with stories about his adventures with Alexa. They helped him gather ferns and flowers to spread over her grave. Betty and Bruce confessed to Matthew that his stories were turning them on. Betty unbuttoned her blouse. She wasn't wearing a bra. Matthew's dick stiffened at the sight of her upturned pink nipples.

Betty kneeled down on the ground and undid Matthew's zipper. He watched her pretty golden head lean forward. As she took his cock in her mouth, Bruce unzipped his pants and stroked his hard cock over the grave. Matthew played with Betty's firm young tits as she pressed her cunt into the soft hallowed ground. Matthew couldn't believe what a good cocksucker she was.

Somehow he wasn't really surprised. For the first time in

years a woman had her hands on him. It felt so damn good. He reached down to touch his cock, glorying to find it so erect and hard. Bruce took his turn in her mouth while Matthew jacked himself off and watched the couple. Their passion for each other turned him on even more. Matthew's fingers entered her cunt while she sucked Bruce. She licked Bruce's cock for a while and then brought her lips back to Matthew's cock. She alternated between the two men. They both screamed out as her lips, tongue, and hands brought them to orgasm. Their cum spilled out onto Alexa's grave and mingled with Betty's cum. The air was full of the scent of sex. Matthew hoped Alexa could smell it and hear their moans. He hoped wherever she was, she was watching, pleasuring right along with them all.

THE DINNER PARTY

Remittance Girl

I

The invitation to dinner was unexpected. It came in the form of an email.

It was very nice to meet you at the Consulate party on Tuesday night. Carmen and I are having a little dinner party on Friday and would be happy if you could join us. We realize that our villa is a little bit out of the way, and getting back to the city might be a problem. Please feel free to use one of our guest rooms.

Drinks at seven p.m. Dinner at nine. Map attached. Please RSVP.

Gilles and Carmen Masé

Isabel opened the map on her phone. "A little bit out of the way" was an understatement. It was in the middle of nowhere, almost forty kilometers north of Ho Chi Minh City, past the old rubber plantations around Bien Hoa.

It wasn't just the distance that made Isabel hesitate. She didn't know these people. They were part of a cliquish French expat community that rarely socialized beyond their own kind. The French still mourned for the days when they'd been colonial masters here, and regularly got together to complain about how everything had turned to shit since they got kicked out.

Still, the invitation intrigued her. Gilles Masé was the owner of a huge lacquerware export company, and Isabel had been bidding for a contract to provide translation services to his company for the last three weeks. It would be stupid not to accept the invitation.

The traffic out of the city was light. The taxi driver was chatty and he assured her that he knew where he was going, but as soon as they turned off the highway and onto a poorly lit dirt track that ran alongside a never-ending row of towering rubber trees, Isabel began to have her doubts. There was nothing out here but run-down shacks that served as housing for the rubber tappers.

"Are you sure you know where the place is?" asked Isabel.

"No problem. The map is good. Just five kilometers up this road and then turn left."

Another five kilometers of this potholed, bumpy road, and Isabel was sure she'd be sick. She wound down the window and let in the warm, humid night air. She could only imagine how hard it would be to get down this track in the rainy season. Why on earth had they chosen to live all the way out here?

After close calls with a three-legged dog, a trio of drunken lads staggering along the verge arm in arm, and a clutch of chickens, they reached the end of the main road and turned left. Isabel could hardly believe her eyes. The gates to the house were over ten feet high, and beyond it, rows of flaming torches picked out a long, straight path to a sprawling white villa.

The gate was open and a number of cars were parked in a row along the drive. Their drivers were playing cards on the hoods of their vehicles or dozing in the front seats.

Isabel paid the taxi driver. "Can you come back for me at eleven o'clock? I don't think I'll be able to find a taxi out here."

The taxi driver looked unenthusiastic. "I don't know. It's a long way to come again."

"I'll pay you double. Please. Otherwise, how will I get home?"

"I'll try to come. Depends on how busy I am. It's Friday, you know."

Isabel shrugged and smiled. "Well, please try," she said, and stepped out of the car.

The grounds and the house were so grand, Isabel suddenly worried that she was underdressed in her plain white linen shift. She'd pulled her hair back in a braid and donned a pair of strappy bronze sandals. Her intention had been to dress sensibly and conservatively. After all, who hires a flamboyant translator? But now, as she walked up the path, she felt she should have made more of an effort. It was a dinner party, after all.

As she walked up the terracotta steps to the broad entrance, Gilles Masé stood waiting, sporting a plain white shirt and linen trousers. Isabel breathed a sigh of relief.

"Isabel! So nice of you to come." He bent and kissed her on both cheeks in the French manner. "Did you have trouble finding us?"

The building was *u*-shaped, and he guided her through the

entrance that led, not to any interior room, but out into a huge courtyard, flanked by the walls of the house, filled with potted plants of every variety and ending at the foot of a wide, aquamarine swimming pool. Isabel was speechless. She'd never seen anything like this in all her years in Saigon. Now she understood why they chose to live here, so far from the city.

"Mr. Masé, what a marvelous house you have."

He smiled at her, looking genuinely pleased by the compliment, even though he must have heard it a thousand times. "Gilles, please. And thank you, it was my grandfather's house. *Je l'ai reprise.*"

Isabel was tempted to ask how he managed to persuade the communist government to let him "take it back," but decided the question was impolitic.

A group of six people stood around, chatting, glasses in their hands. Gilles made the introductions, but the only person Isabel recognized was Gilles's wife, Carmen. She looked cool and elegant and beautiful with her black hair in a tight chignon and a blood-red strapless dress. Carmen Masé was a consummate Parisian woman: svelte, willowy, and always turned out to perfection. Isabel suspected she was Gilles's second wife; she was much younger and had all the signs of being someone's trophy.

Her bracelets jangled as she transferred her drink from one hand to the other and air-kissed Isabel's cheeks. "Wonderful to see you, my dear." She bent and whispered in Isabel's ear, "It's good to have some new blood in our midst. All these boring old colons—I've had enough of them."

The remark surprised Isabel, but it also made her feel less like an interloper in this tightly knit group that had known each other for years, perhaps generations.

The other guests were all older than Isabel: Mr. and Mrs.

Charles Fournier were in their sixties and looked like they'd been married so long they'd begun to resemble each other. Sophie and Marcel d'Aubigne were about the same age as Gilles, perhaps early fifties.

The only other single member of the party was Michél Godard. Although she'd never met him, Isabel had seen him around town. He ran a French bar down in the center of Saigon. In his forties and rather short and stout, he had the pinkish complexion of someone with hypertension. He smirked at Isabel and offered his hand. "I've met you before, I'm sure."

"Not formally. But I've seen you. You run *La Fourchette*, don't you?"

Michél smiled and then pursed his lips. "I do! But I cannot believe that I would have allowed a woman as beautiful as you to come into my establishment without wanting to know her name." He took Isabel's hand and clutched it, covering it with the other. His palms were unpleasantly sweaty and hot.

Isabel did her best not to recoil. "Perhaps you were busy playing dominos at the bar," she said dryly.

He seemed unwilling to let her go, even as Carmen came over bearing a cocktail glass with something suspiciously pink in it. Isabel took the opportunity to free herself and reached for the glass. "Thank you so much," she said, with unseemly emphasis.

Carmen cocked an eyebrow. "Would you like to help me in the kitchen?"

"Of course! I'd love to."

Carmen took her hand and led her into the house and through to an enormous and ancient kitchen where three elderly Vietnamese ladies were hard at work preparing what looked like a banquet. Carmen was in no need of help.

"I must apologize for Michél. His wife left him a year ago and went back to France. He's been unbearably predatory ever since."

Isabel laughed. "Well, thank you for the rescue. He's very friendly but a little . . . as you say."

"It's your white dress," said Carmen, stepping closer. She ran a red-tipped finger along the line of Isabel's shoulder. "He has a thing for virgins."

It was an uncomfortably intimate gesture, and Isabel wasn't certain how to read it. She shrugged and laughed it off. "Well, I'm absolutely safe then."

Carmen giggled and withdrew her hand. "I need to check the dining room, will you come with me?"

"Certainly."

Isabel followed her through a pair of massive wooden doors, past a darkened salon and out onto a wide wooden veranda. A table was set in the middle. It glowed in the dim light; its white tablecloth and glinting silverware reflected the flames from a pair of lit candelabras.

"Your house is just gorgeous, Carmen."

Carmen walked around the table, checking settings, moving a glass, refolding a napkin. "Yes," she murmured distractedly, "but it is very lonely out here."

"I'd imagine it is."

The woman stopped and smiled, her face framed on either side by the flickering tapers. "My husband, he likes you."

Good god, the French are weird, thought Isabel. It was a simple statement but she had no idea how to decipher this woman. Isabel decided that it was safer to take her words at face value. "I'm very glad to hear it. I was hoping to get his translation work."

Carmen shrugged her elegant, angular shoulders. Her tanned

skin looked coppery in the candlelight. "Oh, I'm sure you'll get that," she said, lightly.

Seated around the table, their conversation was animated and in French. Although Isabel was fluent, it was not her first language and she listened to the banter feeling like a spy. She was being afforded a glimpse into this closed-off world of people who dreamt of the past and regretted the present.

Gilles Masé sat at the head of the table, playing the magnanimous host. He lounged back, one arm carelessly flung over the back of his chair. In his other hand, he held a half-empty glass of Beaujolais. He was a bigger man than she remembered, and his hair was shot through with silver strands. He had a strong neck, a very square jaw, and rather intense brown eyes. He was handsome in an arrogant, paternal sort of way. From time to time, his eyes rested on Isabel, as if assessing her. It made her uncomfortable, and she took refuge in the chatty Michél who was sitting opposite.

Carmen was on Gilles's left, showing the effects of having drunk a little too much. She brushed her glass with her hand and knocked it over, spilling deep red liquid onto the pristine tablecloth. It spread out like blood.

"Oh, how clumsy!" she giggled, trying to staunch the spread with her napkin.

"You did it on purpose, Carmen."

It was Gilles's voice, hard and cold, totally unlike the easy-going bonhomie of his earlier conversations. The change was unaccountably abrupt; Isabel felt a small chill run down her spine. The whole table fell silent.

"I . . . I didn't!" Carmen pleaded, unable to keep the laughter out of her voice.

"Don't argue, Carmen. Stand up," Gilles said, getting

up himself. The legs of his chair scraped against the wooden flooring.

Carmen stopped twittering. "No . . . no, Gilles. I'll get the maids to change the cloth. Just wait a moment. I can make it all . . ."

"Stand. Up." The voice was clipped and cruel; it was a voice that would not tolerate dissention.

Isabel sat paralyzed. In all her life, she'd never heard a man talk to his wife that way in front of other people. Suddenly, she felt very protective of Carmen. "Gilles," she said quietly, but firmly, "It's just a little spilled wine. I'll help clean it up." She started to rise, but the dangerous look in Gilles's eyes stopped her.

Across the table, Michél reached out and took her hand, pinning it to the cloth. "Don't interfere, Isabel. They do this all the time."

Down at the end of the table, Carmen rose slowly to her feet, and began to move her place setting to the side. She did it in slow motion, like an automaton, until the table in front of her was entirely clear of everything but the dark, red stain.

"Bend over."

Isabel's jaw dropped open as she watched this beautiful, sophisticated woman bend over the table until her upper body was resting on it.

"This kind of undisciplined behavior is unacceptable," said Gilles quietly.

"Yes, *Maître,*" Carmen said.

Isabel watched the woman's face lying on its side against the wine stain. Her lips were almost exactly the same color. They moved, but her eyes were glazed over and dead.

"How dare you embarrass me in front of my guests. Apologize this instant."

"Yes, *Maître*. I apologize for my behavior." Carmen's voice was toneless and as dead as her eyes. Then, slowly she closed them.

If it hadn't been for the fact that she was stuck in the middle of nowhere, with her hand pinned to the table in Michél's sweaty grip, Isabel would have walked out. The whole scene was surreal. These people were all surely insane. This was like watching a car crash in slow motion. Isabel didn't want to be here. She didn't want to be a witness to this—whatever it was.

Finally, she got up the nerve to speak again. "Gilles, please stop this. There is no need for an apology. It was just a glass of wine, for god's sake!"

But Gilles wasn't listening. He reached down and pulled the hem of Carmen's red dress over her hips. Beneath, the woman wore nothing. Her bare buttocks gleamed in the candlelight.

"Be quiet, Isabel," hissed Michél. "Don't spoil the fun. This is the only reason I bother coming out to the godforsaken place!"

"You're all crazy," Isabel hissed back. "This is barbarous!"

Mrs. Fournier, who had said nothing up until now, looked over at Isabel and giggled. "It's nothing more than she deserves, my dear."

The sound of flesh hitting flesh made Isabel jump and lock her eyes on the source of the noise. The first slap moved Carmen's body farther onto the table and set the glasses and dishes tinkling. The woman herself was completely silent.

Gilles drew his hand back to smack her again, and Isabel heard someone inhale sharply. The second slap made Carmen yelp. Isabel saw the pain of the blow flash through her face before leaving it, once more, eerily expressionless.

She felt Michél let go of her hand. He drew it beneath the table and she heard the distinct sound of a fly being unzipped.

The whole thing was beyond description. As the spanking

continued, Carmen's cries became louder and louder. But the woman didn't struggle or try to get away. In fact, despite the noise she was making, she was clearly enjoying this. She'd pulled her hands beneath her chest, and was squeezing her own breasts as the castigation went on.

Gilles, on the other hand, was unreadable. He dealt out the punishment with studied impassivity. Over and over, he hit the lovely upturned buttocks with the broad palm of his hand, leaving visible prints on his wife's flesh.

A little worm of excitement curled and twisted in Isabel's stomach. She knew she should get up and leave; what she was witnessing defied all appropriate behavior. She fought the strange feeling, willing herself to turn her eyes away from the terrible, fascinating spectacle. Then, just as she thought she'd overcome her unaccountable reluctance to move, the spanking stopped.

It was impossible to ignore the groans and sighs and quick breathing that filled the silence around the table. At the head of it, Gilles smoothed a possessive hand over Carmen's red bottom.

"*Eh bien, mon petite. C'est fini.*"

Mr. d'Aubigne made a disappointed sound. "You can't leave her like that, Gilles. It's unkind. You have to finish her off."

Isabel's back went rigid. She scanned the faces round the table in disbelief. "Finish her off? Are you all out of your minds?" she demanded.

Gilles chuckled, his hand still rubbing his wife's rump. "I suppose it doesn't sound very appealing in translation," he said in English. And, without taking his eyes off Isabel's face, he slid his hand between his wife's buttocks and began to caress her. Even at a distance of ten feet, Isabel could hear his fingers slipping through the wet flesh of his wife's cunt. Carmen moaned and arched her back, beginning to pant. And, even from her vantage point, Isabel knew when he'd pushed his fingers inside her, because the posture of Carmen's body changed and she began to push backward, riding his fingers.

Despite her intentions, Isabel's own body responded to what she was witnessing. Between her legs, her panties were dampening, and as she moved, uncomfortably, in her chair, her inner thighs were slick with her own juices. Carmen's moans and grunts added to the bizarre eroticism of it all. And, around the table, people cleared their throats, and fidgeted in their seats. Mr. and Mrs. d'Aubigne began to kiss deeply, passionately.

Isabel tried to look anywhere but at Gilles Masé, but every time her gaze drifted back to him, he was staring at her, even as his wife impaled herself on his fingers. Isabel felt her face turn red and she forced herself to stare down at the empty plate in front of her, until Carmen moaned and began to shudder so hard the whole table shook.

"Ah! *Je jouis. Je jouis!*" stuttered Carmen. Her body relaxed, and her eyes closed.

Then it was over. It seemed as if everyone let out a sigh. Carmen pushed herself up off the table, smoothed a couple of stray wisps of hair from her face, and primly pulled down her dress.

Isabel considered the problem of getting up from the table. How was she going to hide what felt like a massive damp spot on the seat of her dress? Why couldn't she have worn black?

"We have strawberries and crème fraiche for dessert. Does everyone want some?" asked Carmen.

Isabel, who couldn't for the life of her decide how to respond properly to what she'd just witnessed, gave a mute nod.

II

Isabel ate her strawberries in silence. The table had seemingly returned to normal. It had been cleared in silence by one of the Masé's staff and the tablecloth replaced; even the wine stain was gone. The conversation had reverted back to gossip and rumor: whose business was doing well, who was leaving for the home country, which was the best international school. Isabel pretended to listen, but her mind was still trapped at the moment when Carmen's face grew still and her body slumped, sated, against the stained white cloth.

It was difficult to understand why each of these seemingly conservative, middle-class couples sat silently, watching a performance of what Isabel considered to be, at the very least, the private sexual peccadilloes of a husband and wife. Now they were acting as if nothing out of the ordinary had happened. Worse yet, the uncomfortable twinges between Isabel's legs hadn't abated. She could still feel herself oozing all over the back of her dress. Now—while everyone was busy with dessert and coffee—was a good time to find a bathroom and see what could be done about it.

"Could you tell me where your bathroom is?" she asked Carmen.

"It's through the salon and to your right. Shall I come with you?"

"No . . . no. It's fine. I'm sure I'll find it."

"Are you sure?" Carmen asked, standing up.

Isabel felt a moment of panic. She had no desire for company or for having to discuss her state of disarray. "No," she said again, rather too loudly. "I'm absolutely certain I'll be just fine. Thanks anyway."

She stood up, backed away from the table as gracefully as she could, and made a rather awkward sideways exit into the darkened living room. It wasn't hard to find the bathroom; it was through a door in the small hallway that connected the living room to the kitchen.

Once inside, she switched on the light and turned to lock the door, but there was no lock, so she closed it firmly and stood with her back to the mirror above the sink, trying to survey the damage. It wasn't as bad as she'd feared. If she kept standing up, and let it dry, the stain would not be noticeable. Her panties, however, were another matter. They felt tacky and unpleasant between her legs. Isabel reached beneath her dress and stepped out of them, then filled the sink with water and began to rinse them out. If she rolled them in a towel to get the excess dampness out of them, they'd dry quickly.

As she washed them, her mind kept creeping back to the earlier scene at the table. She shook her head and tried to think of day-to-day things, but the sound of the slaps against bare skin and Carmen moaning her way to orgasm kept echoing in her head. When she looked up at herself in the sink's mirror, she was sweating and flushed. The need to masturbate, to be rid of this overwhelming urge, was so great it felt impossible to bear. Perhaps if she just gave herself an orgasm, she'd feel less trapped, less disassociated. It wouldn't take her long.

Pulling up the hem of her skirt, she thrust a hand between her legs, bracing herself against the wall with the other. Her fingers were cool and wet and the shock of them against her swollen labia made her shiver. She bit her lip so as not to make a noise and began to work with dedicated concentration. The images of the evening flooded back into her mind, and this time she didn't stop them. Isabel closed her eyes and pushed her fingers between the slick lips of her cunt, grazing her clit over and over with her fingertips and teasing them into her hole with every pass.

She imagined herself on that table, in Carmen's place. It wasn't the audience that excited her; it was the sensation, the vulnerability, the sting, and the hot flush. She was halfway there.

"May I be of some assistance?"

The voice made her jump and her eyes flashed open. She'd half expected Carmen to come knocking at the door to see if she was okay, but she hadn't expected Gilles.

He closed the door behind him before she had a chance to object. He stepped behind her quickly and engulfed her, pushing her hand out of the way, replacing it with his own.

"My god," Isabel stuttered. "This . . . this . . . this isn't right." But even as she said it, she felt a new flood of juice seeping out around his thick, rough fingers.

The hand that was not busy pushing its way into her cunt covered her mouth. "Can you smell her on my hand?" he whispered. "Do you like it? Just her smell alone is enough to make me come."

Isabel whimpered and inhaled deep. She could indeed smell the cloying, rich scent of Carmen on his fingers. Moaning, she parted her lips and tasted the skin of his hand.

"She likes you," he panted into her ear as he began to fuck her with two fingers. "She wants you to stay. And I want what she wants, always."

She let her head fall back against his chest and felt the faint spasms begin.

"Stay. Will you stay?" He thrust another finger inside her and pushed her over the edge.

"Yes," Isabel moaned. Her voice muffled by his hand, by Carmen's scent, by her own lust.

She jerked against him, repeatedly, like a marionette with taut, directed strings. His hips were pressed against her ass, his hard cock upright and nestled between her buttocks. She couldn't stop coming. His fingers curled forward, brushing her G-spot and she convulsed, the muscles of her passage walls clamped, like an iris shutting, and ached around his fingers.

"Do you want my cock?"

Isabel shook her head. "No, please . . . enough," she mumbled.

"Later, then," he said.

He slowly pulled his fingers out of her, leaving an empty, deflated feeling behind. In the mirror, she saw him raise them to his mouth and suck them clean. Isabel stood on trembling legs as the blood returned to her muscles, twitching as the little aftershocks raced through her body. It was all she could do not to collapse in a puddle on the floor.

Gilles looked down into the sink at the white silk panties floating in the water. "Don't bother with those. You won't need them around here."

III

Isabel walked mutely back onto the dining veranda. It was irrational, but she was positive that they only had to take one look at her face to know what she'd just been doing. If they didn't see it, they'd smell it—she was sure.

But Mr. and Mrs. d'Aubigne were on their feet, with Michél beside them, saying their good nights. With what seemed like a little more reluctance, Mr. and Mrs. Fournier did the same. Carmen was being a perfect hostess, protesting that they were leaving far too early, but Isabel could hear the lack of conviction in her words.

"Must you go? Oh, how sad. Won't you stay for a cognac?"

"No. It's a long way back to town, my dear," said Madame Fournier. "Next time, you must come to us."

Michél stepped away from the crowd and cornered Isabel. "It was such a pleasure to meet you. I'm sure we'll meet again very soon."

"It was very nice. Yes, I'm sure we'll run into each other.

Saigon can be such a small place." Isabel made a mental note that *La Fourchette* was now strictly out of bounds.

"Well, you know where I am. You can find me any night of the week."

"I certainly do," replied Isabel.

Mr. d'Aubigne joined their group, smiling. "Would you like to ride with us back into town? We have a big car and lots of room. You aren't going to find a taxi out here at this time of night."

"Well," hesitated Isabel. "It's very kind of you to offer, but . . ."

A light hand fell on her shoulder. "But Isabel is staying with us for the weekend. She and Gilles have a mountain of translation work to do." Carmen casually put her arm around Isabel's shoulder and gave it a friendly squeeze. "Don't you?"

Isabel blushed. "Oh, yes. Mountains," she agreed, feeling slightly sheepish.

Michél and Monsieur d'Aubigne gave each other an enigmatic glance. Something that Isabel couldn't discern passed between them.

"Well, that's wonderful then. Everyone's set," chirped Michél, grabbing Isabel's hand and kissing her messily on both cheeks. Before he pulled away, he pressed his lips to her ear and hissed, "I'd love to see you two together, eating each other up."

Isabel tugged her hand out of his grasp. She couldn't think of anything more disgusting than performing for this repulsive slug of a man. The thought made her cringe. Before she could get the words of disdain she was planning for him out of her mouth, Carmen slid her arm through Isabel's and pulled her away, through the house and out onto the front steps of the entryway.

The guests were repeating their good nights, the way all

guests will. Carmen held Isabel's arm possessively and watched the guests get into their cars. Gilles was talking to the drivers, giving them directions to get back to the highway in rather halting, French-accented Vietnamese.

"Smile and wave," Carmen muttered. "Smile and wave." Her fingers brushed discreetly against the side of Isabel's breast as she watched them off.

Isabel, not knowing quite what else to do, did what she was told: she smiled and waved.

As the last of the cars had driven through the gates, Carmen turned to Isabel, wrapped her arms around her, and kissed her hard on the mouth. The ferocity of the kiss startled Isabel. She'd never kissed a woman before and she hadn't expected anything so forceful.

"Thank god. I thought they'd never leave," murmured Carmen.

She kissed Isabel again, softer this time and Isabel found it impossible not to respond. The woman's lips were so soft, so lush, and beneath the scent of her perfume, Isabel could smell the fragrance that had so overwhelmed her in the bathroom.

She relaxed in Carmen's arms and drew her own around the woman, opening her mouth to Carmen's inquisitive tongue, tasting wine and strawberries; it was heady and addictive. Isabel sucked at it, as if she could consume and incorporate the very essence of Carmen that way.

"What a lovely picture you make."

Isabel pulled away from the kiss. She was unsure of how something like this unfolded. Of course, she'd read all sorts of novels where three people were involved, but they were romantic and full of drama and jealousy. This was about skin and need and something quite indefinable. But something in the back of Isabel's mind made her cautious.

"We're hot, Gilles," said Carmen, in a pouting, little girl's voice. She pressed her warm cheek against Isabel's. "We want to swim. Don't we?"

Isabel giggled and nodded. She could feel the faint pulse in Carmen's throat through the woman's skin.

"Who am I to deny two beautiful ladies their desires?" Carmen laughed. "Will you watch, *Maître?*"

"*Mais oui, naturellement.* Let me grab a cognac."

They shed their clothes as they walked through the courtyard. Isabel watched as Carmen unzipped her red dress and pulled it down, leaving it in a puddle on the tiles.

"You're . . ." Isabel paused to find the words. For someone who had spent her whole life using words as tools, she was struggling to find the right ones now. Instead she reached out and laid a hesitant hand over one of Carmen's breasts. "Very beautiful."

Carmen laughed and shrugged. She reached up to unpin her hair. It tumbled down around her bare shoulders in dark cascades. Beneath her palm, Isabel felt the nipple stiffen.

"And what are you?" Carmen asked. She placed a hand on top of Isabel's and squeezed. "Let's see if you're a mermaid. Come into the water."

The pool shimmered electric blue as they waded in. The chill made Isabel's breath catch in her throat. Cool eddies swirled around her thighs and, as she moved farther in, her hips. She shivered.

"Come," whispered Carmen, pulling her closer. She wrapped her arms around Isabel's waist and crushed their bodies together.

Isabel looked down. There was something painfully erotic about seeing their breasts pressed together, their nipples touching. Drawing Carmen's face to hers, she pressed her lips against the woman's mouth. Inhaling her breath again. There was something magical about her skin. Once her lips were in contact with it, it was so hard to break away. She trailed her parted lips over Carmen's cheek and down her neck. The body in her arms shuddered as she opened her mouth and sucked at the skin.

"Isabel," Gilles's voice called from the side of the pool. "You must kiss her breasts. They're exquisitely sensitive."

Nodding, Isabel wrapped her arms around Carmen's waist, lifting her up in the water. She gazed at one perfectly petite breast, watching the mulberry-colored nipple crinkle and stiffen in anticipation. Isabel covered her mouth with it, sucking it gently and dragging her tongue over the hard, ridged nub. Carmen moaned and arched her back, pressing more of herself into Isabel's mouth.

Splashing in the water made Isabel open her eyes. Gilles was wading into the pool, his shirt undone, but otherwise fully dressed. He stopped beside them, a balloon glass of brandy in one hand.

"Bite it. She loves it."

Isabel grazed Carmen's nipple with her teeth, then bit it tenderly. Carmen's body stiffened and twitched in her arms. She bit again, harder this time, and was rewarded with another sharper twitch and a guttural moan.

Gilles draped his arm around Isabel's shoulders and brought his lips to her ear. The sensation of his breath on her skin turned it to gooseflesh.

"Harder," he whispered, and then kissed her ear. "Don't be scared to hurt her."

Isabel mewed and pressed her teeth into Carmen's flesh until she was worried that she'd break the skin. The effect was immediate: the woman in her arms bucked her hips and whimpered. She wrapped her legs tight around Isabel's hips and began to grind herself shamelessly against Isabel's pelvic bone. What would it be like to have a cock and fuck her this way, Isabel wondered. She dropped her gaze to watch Carmen's hips roll against her in the water.

Gilles finished off his brandy, waded to the side of the pool, and left the glass. When he returned, he put his arms around both of them.

"Carmen loves sex. Don't you, my little *salope?* She'll rub herself raw against anything if you're not careful." Gilles grabbed Carmen by the waist and lifted her onto the side of the pool. "Show Isabel your ravenous little cunt."

Carmen brushed her hair off her face, her expression one of impatience and need. She spread her legs wide. Isabel waded over to them, fascinated. She'd never seen any woman's pussy but her own, in the mirror. Carmen was shaved, and her outer lips were plump and blood-engorged. Her clit peeked out from between her inner folds, fuchsia, like a beacon, the same size as her erect nipples.

With a single finger, Gilles reached between Carmen's thighs and stroked the prominent clit with one fingertip. His wife reacted by splaying her legs wider still and leaning back on her elbows; letting her head drop backward, she arched her hips. She growled like a cat in heat.

"Want to taste?" Gilles asked.

Isabel moved between Carmen's legs, stroking her thighs until her face was level with Carmen's pussy. She'd never done this before, but she knew this terrain well enough; how delicious it felt to be pleasured this way. Lowering her mouth onto Carmen's mound, Isabel stroked her tongue along the length of her slit. She began to tease the hard, erect bud with the tip of her tongue, unhooding it, giving it attention, and then returning to long, languid laps.

Gilles moved behind her and wrapped his arms around her, cupping her tits, teasing the nipples. Isabel moaned into Carmen's pussy and began to suck rhythmically at her clit, dragging her tongue over the nub every so often, until Carmen began to make plaintive, begging sounds. Then, with one swift movement, she pushed two fingers deep into Carmen's cunt. The slicked walls fluttered and contracted around her fingers. Isabel sucked harder, and pushed her fingers deeper, fucking as she feasted.

"Ah, Maître. Permettre-moi, je vous prie!" Carmen whimpered.

Behind her, Gilles laughed. "She wants to come. Should we let her?"

Isabel nodded. "I think so," she whispered against Carmen's clit.

Carmen was coming. Her hips, perfectly still until now, bucked beneath Isabel's mouth, fucking herself with Isabel's fingers. A flood of juices seeped from her slit, drenching Isabel's mouth and hand. It was just like she remembered, when she tasted Gilles's fingers—sweet, musky, and tangy.

Carmen roared and convulsed. Her legs shook with the strength of her orgasm. Then, as it abated, she lay back on the edge of the pool and sighed into the night sky. Isabel thought it was the most beautiful thing she'd ever witnessed.

"Kiss me," said Gilles, pulling Isabel back into the center of the pool. He turned her around in the water. "Kiss me."

Isabel put her arms around his shoulders and kissed him, her face and lips slick with Carmen's juices. He sucked her tongue into his mouth and fed off it, holding her head in his hands, as if she were a piece of fruit for him to devour. When he pulled away, he looked at her and smiled.

"Nothing tastes as good as my wife on another woman's lips."

IV

"Carmen, go inside and prepare the necessaries."

Carmen lazily drew her legs together and stood up. "Perhaps you should ask her first, *Maître?*"

Gilles laughed and looked at Isabel. "It did not occur to me that our guest is . . ." He traced the tips of his fingers around the swell of one of her breasts, just at the waterline. "A little shy perhaps, but not unwilling. *N'est-ce pas?*"

Before Isabel could answer, Carmen pressed the point. "Ask her, Gilles." And, beautiful and lithe in the blue glow of the pool, she turned on her heels and disappeared into the darkness of the house's overhang.

"Come," he said, leading Isabel by the hand, out of the water. "We have work to do also."

"Ask me what?" said Isabel, allowing herself to be led. She followed him, dripping water as she went, across the cool tiles of the courtyard, toward the kitchen.

The room was now, to Isabel's relief, empty of staff. She stood in the middle of the kitchen, hugging her arms to her chest. "What should you ask me, Gilles?"

He stood with his back to her, preparing something on a tray. Turning with a lychee fruit in his hand, he peeled it and held it up to her. "Do you like lychees?"

Isabel made to take the peeled fruit from his hand, but he pulled it away, teasing her.

"Carmen says they feel like the head of a cock."

Gilles touched the round, firm fruit to her lips, sliding it back and forth, painting them with its juice. He nodded encouragingly when she opened her mouth, clasping the dripping white fruit in her mouth. A trickle of juice escaped, ran over her chin and down her neck. Putting a hand to her face, he covered her mouth with the palm, crushing the fruit against her teeth and pressing it inwards. His warm mouth went to her neck, where the single dribble had become a stream of sticky juice as the fruit exploded.

Isabel moaned, almost choking as the juice flooded her mouth. The sensation of his tongue on her throat made her cunt flood in response.

Gilles stood back, wiping the juice off his face with the back of his hand. "*Chassez-tu le dragon,* Isabel?"

Isabel took her time answering, swallowing the rest of the lychee flesh, and spitting the round black pit out into her hand. "Hunt the what?"

"Have you ever smoked opium?"

"No. I've smoked weed, but not opium."

"It's very different." He turned back to face her, carrying a tray with all sorts of things on it: a carafe of water, fruit, a bowl of ice, a small, silver knife. "Would you like to try?" He left the kitchen, heading through the darkened house.

Everyone in Vietnam had read something about opium. It had been the scourge of the Mandarin class under the French. Some historians suggested that the French colonial authorities sold it to them cheap, on purpose, to erode their power and sense of independence.

"What's it like?" Isabel called after him, following him through the semidarkness.

"It's like heaven."

"But . . . isn't it addictive?"

His laugh echoed off the dark walls as he led the way down a dimly lit hallway. "Certainly it is, if you overindulge. But then," he stopped before a pair of large oak doors. Turning, he pushed them open with his shoulder, careful not to upset the tray, ". . . so is Carmen."

The bedroom was cavernous. One wall was lined with louvered doors, open and overlooking the courtyard. But what dominated the room was the bed, a huge, low piece of furniture— an old-fashioned Vietnamese sleeping platform big enough for a whole family. The bed had been covered with a mattress and each corner was posted with a towering polished wooded post. Gauzy white netting cascaded down from each one.

Carmen lay stretched out on her side. She looked up from what she was doing as they came in. "Are you all right with this, Isabel?"

Nearing the bed, Isabel could see that Carmen was playing the end of a long, thin needle through the flame of a small burner. There was a marble-sized glob of something dark and viscose on the end of the skewer.

Isabel watched, fascinated. "I . . . I'm not sure. I think I am."

"Did Gilles explain?" Carmen asked, patting an empty spot on the huge white bed.

Hesitating a little, Isabel took a seat on the edge of the bed. Despite all the previous intimacy, she felt a little out of place, like an interloper here. It seemed ridiculous, considering that beneath the taste of lychee, her mouth still held the ghost of Carmen's flavor. "He said it was like heaven."

"*Bête!*" teased Carmen, poking a polished toe into Gilles's side. "You did not tell her everything." She sat up and trans-ferred her attention back to her preparations. The blob of opium was now less solid. She picked up a pipe that lay beside her and skillfully deposited the dollop into the saucer-like ceramic bowl of the pipe.

"The first time you smoke it, it can make you a little nauseous. But it soon passes." Gilles took the pipe from Carmen and stretched out on his side. His deep brown skin looked African against the whiteness of the sheets. Holding the pipe with both hands—one at the mouthpiece and one almost at the end—he inhaled deeply as Carmen held the burner at the pipe's bowl, waving the flame back and forth. He took short, deep sips of the pipe, then after holding the vapor in his lungs for a few seconds, exhaled a long, thick stream of smoke. Then he drew on it again, this time deeply, causing the pipe to bubble. He held the smoke in for even longer and nodded, smiling.

The room took on a sweet, acrid smell, like over-ripe fruit and smoldering pinewood.

"Encore, Maître?" asked Carmen.

Gilles shook his head, offering the pipe to Isabel. "A full bowl is not easy to take. Have the rest of this one."

Isabel took the pipe, and feeling a little silly, held it to her lips.

"Lie down or you will fall down, *mon petite.*"

She nodded and moved back, leaning on her hip, with her head resting on the bolster at the foot of the bed.

"When you draw, you will want to cough, but don't," whispered Carmen. The woman tilted the end of the pipe a bit and brought the flame to the bowl. "Now . . . suck it in just like *Maître* did."

Isabel took three quick puffs in succession. The smoke didn't feel like a cigarette; it was infinitely thicker. Her lungs fought to hold the vapor and her eyes watered as she tried not to cough. When it was too much, she expelled huge gouts of smoke, spluttering.

"Again, *vite!*" Carmen pressed the mouthpiece back against Isabel's lips.

Obediently, Isabel again drew on the pipe. This time, as soon as the smoke hit her lungs, she felt a creeping tingle that began at the soles of her feet and crept up the back of her thighs. It spread over her buttocks and pooled at the base of her spine.

"Oh my god," muttered Isabel, still struggling to keep the smoke inside. But her lungs burned and convulsed and the smoke came streaming out as she gave up the fight.

It felt as if a huge, heavy snake had coiled itself around her loins and began to squeeze. The embrace inched up her body, making her nipples stiffen and ache as it passed over them. Suddenly, in a rush, it raced up her neck and pushed into her head.

"My . . . my . . . oh . . ." Isabel closed her eyes.

A cold frozen cube pressed against her lips. She mewed and felt the cold slip into her mouth.

"Suck the ice and breathe through your nose." Carmen's voice seemed a long way away.

Something awful and huge lurched in Isabel's stomach. She opened her eyes and tried to speak around the icecube. Urgently, she spat it out into her hand.

"I'm . . . I'm going to be sick," she said, panicked, trying to sit upright.

An arm surrounded her—Carmen's—and cool, moist fingers smoothed the hair away from her face. "No, no *ma petite*. It will pass. Just breathe deeply and . . ."

Carmen pressed the ice cube back into Isabel's mouth. "It's just the dragon's tail swishing about. It will pass."

And it did. After a short time, Isabel began to feel better, sleepier, and the snake inside her pushed into her face and made her smile. She giggled inanely, hearing her own laughter echo in a deep well. "I'm okay. I'm okay now. Thank you, Carmen."

The woman smiled back and set about preparing the pipe for herself. Isabel watched through half-lidded eyes as Carmen smoked, and then Gilles, and then Carmen. Finally, in what seemed to Isabel like slow motion, Carmen pushed the tray of implements away and stretched herself out on the bed.

V

It was impossible to say how long they lay silent, drifting through layers of dream. Images would flood into Isabel's mind, swallowing her up and then release her with the taste of them lingering on her tongue; joy, sadness, loneliness, ecstasy were all flavors. She was a child looking up at a gray sky, gentle snowflakes falling on her face. And then she was in water as thick as honey, pushing through velvet caves with glinting, gold-flecked walls, like a mermaid. Vermillion anemones extended their fingers and caressed her as she swam by. When she stretched out, she was a pale Luna moth breaking out of its cocoon into the midnight air. She let her wings dry in the cool air currents.

When Carmen kissed her, Isabel still thought she was dreaming. Flowers grew from her tongue as she pushed it into Carmen's mouth. Tendrils of pleasure sprouted from her cheeks, growing upward to embrace the woman in curling, sentient filaments of bliss. Only when she reached to cup Carmen's face did she know it was real. Isabel moaned, pushing wave after wave of desire between Carmen's lips.

Something touched her breasts and the sensation made her arch her back and twist. The mouth that covered one of them was scalding. It couldn't be Carmen's—she was feeding on Carmen's mouth. Each delectable kiss made her hungrier. She could never, ever have enough.

She reached blindly for Carmen's breasts and cradled them in her hands. Above her, they settled like delicate, trembling desserts into her palms. Isabel had to taste them. Her mouth flooded in anticipation; she left off kissing and wriggled across the bed until she could take a berry-like nipple between her lips.

As Isabel fed, the borders between what she was doing

and what was being done to her blurred, for her own breasts throbbed with pleasure beneath an unseen mouth's ministrations. She reached upward, sliding her hand over the woman's undulating belly and delving into Carmen's flooded cunt. Stroking and circling between the wet folds of the woman's sex, she coaxed sublimely wanton sounds from Carmen's throat. She licked and chewed and bit before changing breasts and pushing two fingers deep into Carmen's passage. Catching a nipple again between her teeth, Isabel felt Carmen start to move. Isabel bit down, trapping the erect nub even as Carmen began slowly, deliciously to impale herself on Isabel's fingers. The sounds that Carmen spoke of exquisite pain and pleasure.

Gradually, Isabel became aware of a sensation between her legs. A warm tongue pushed between her nether lips and probed her clit, circling it and dabbing at it, first gently and then more insistently. Each contact sent a Morse code signal to her brain. She spread her thighs eagerly, greedily. She rolled her hips in the warmth of this sweetest of sensations.

Then it was gone. And Carmen stopped moving. Isabel looked down her body to see Gilles kneeling between her spread legs. His dark hair was disheveled, his lips—glinting with her juices—sparkled in the light. Between his thighs rose a very erect cock. He leaned forward and pulled Isabel's hips, sliding them up onto his thighs so that only her shoulders were on the bed. His eyes were almost closed. He took his cock in his hand and began to tease her slit with it, stroking the tip lazily, back and forth over her clit and then down to her opening. Anticipation robbed Isabel of her breath.

She looked up at Carmen, who was smiling. The woman bent forward, until their lips were almost touching and she whispered to Isabel, "Now you understand, yes? How can I not let him rule me? With a cock like that . . ."

Isabel's reply was a whimper.

Even as she pushed another finger into Carmen, even as Gilles grasped her hips and entered her, Isabel listened to the woman's fevered whispers.

"Can you feel him? Can you feel him destroy all your barriers?"

Isabel gasped and nodded her head. Warm tears trickled along the curve of her cheek. She didn't know if they were hers. Her body shifted as he filled her. He settled his hand on her lower belly and pressed his thumb to her clit. Her walls contracted almost painfully around his cock.

"No!" panted Isabel.

"This is what he does. He decimates everything that stands between you and pleasure, and then he owns you."

Carmen pressed her lips to Isabel's. They trembled as she worked herself on Isabel's fingers. She did it in the same slow, determined way that her husband fucked.

Isabel was not a loud lover, but now it felt as if she would explode if she did not cry out. She sobbed into Carmen's mouth. The pleasure would engulf her, she was sure.

"Beg for it . . . scream it, *ma petite,*" stuttered Carmen. "There's . . . nothing better . . . in the world . . ."

Even as Isabel melted, she felt Carmen's cunt constrict around her fingers in sharp waves. The woman groaned and kissed her messily. She felt the shudders ebb away, through Carmen's lips.

"Hold her, Carmen."

"Yes, *Maître.*"

Isabel felt Carmen's hands on her shoulders, pinning her down onto the bed. She could hardly bear the intensity of the pleasure being visited upon her. When Carmen began to kiss her again, it was like the woman was someone else. The lips felt softer, bigger. The tongue that filled her mouth was insistent. It didn't quest; it fucked.

A wave, a terrifying surge began to move up her body. Her body went rigid with its approach. She didn't have control of it any more, it didn't belong to her.

Carmen stopped kissing her and pressed her cheek against Isabel's, cradling Isabel's head in her arms.

"You're going to come, aren't you?" Carmen whispered.

"Ah-h."

"Tell him so. Tell him you love it. It pleases him so much."

Isabel fought to verbalize. It felt like she had lost control of her voice too. She groaned, and closed her eyes, tight. The next thrust exploded in deep russets behind her eyes.

"Coming. God, I'm coming. Gilles . . . I love it." Her words began to tumble out in a whispered torrent. "I love . . ."

"Tell him!"

But she couldn't. She arched her back instead. Pleasure shot through her body, rushing up her spine and erupting from her mouth as a throaty, primal cry.

He doubled over her, taking the flesh of her belly between his teeth, and biting her skin as he came into her.

Isabel twitched over and over. Shocks raced through her torso and, at first, she thought they were aftershocks from her orgasm. Gilles, still buried in her, stroked her sides and bit hard into the flesh of her abdomen.

"Jesus . . ." she whispered, shocked.

She clenched around his cock. "No . . . no . . ."

Gilles groaned and bit her harder.

Isabel was a doll, boneless and unnamed. She shuddered until the spasms of that strange, second orgasm passed.

"Now you know," said Carmen, looking into her face. "Now you understand?"

Isabel nodded.

BECAUSE
OF BINGO

Rebecca M. Kyle

"BINGO!" I'd yelled it so many times I barely had a voice left. Nope, I wasn't a blue-haired little septuagenarian with a brightly colored dauber and a dozen game cards in front of me, delighted I'd won the pot.

I'm a twenty-five-year-old Army widow whose form was obscured in an oversize sweatshirt and Army jacket that used to belong to my husband. I stood on the corner of a busy Austin intersection shivering from the cold, stapling the LOST DOG poster to a utility pole bearing the motley remains of half a dozen pages in various faded colors. My auburn hair was frozen to my head in icy dreadlocks, thanks to a brief sleet storm and freezing temperatures. The longer my golden retriever was lost, the more likely it was he'd not return. My eyes were bleary from crying for hours the day before and not sleeping last night. My throat hurt from calling out his name in near-freezing tempera-tures. I'd driven out at least two tanks of gas yelling out the car window. The reward I offered was a week's salary, which would make living more difficult for a while, but surviving without my dog after I'd lost my husband in Afghanistan fourteen months ago was nothing I wanted to contemplate.

Good thing I gave up on dating and got a dog. From the side-eye folks were giving me, I suspected I looked like a crazy homeless woman. But I'd had it with trying to find someone—from disastrous fix-ups that ended a couple of friendships to the compatibility matches I was certain were the result of computer malfunction or outright deceit on the part of the men filling out the profiles. All that experience taught me was that I was better off alone.

That's when I saw a golden retriever rescue out in front of the HEB and decided to take a look. Bingo was not even a year old. He had belonged to another military family from Fort Hood that'd gotten deployed to Germany and didn't have the financial resources to care for him along with a new set of twins coming. That happened far too often and the animal-friendly community in Austin often helped find homes for former military pets.

I hadn't meant to stop, but I couldn't look in the golden's big brown eyes and walk away. The place we rented allowed one pet, so I took him.

Bingo wasn't perfect company. He hogged the center of the bed, farted enough that I was afraid to light a candle, and snored like a freight train, but he was always glad to see me when I came home from work and he didn't complain about my taste in movies or clothes or . . . anything. We weren't the perfect match, but we were happy.

I never felt so empty as when I saw the back gate open and my dog gone from his toy-littered yard. Had someone taken him? Or had it just been the meter man being forgetful to shut the gate? I'd walked around my neighborhood, yelling myself hoarse, and plastered posters on every utility pole within a few blocks the first day.

Day two, I'd broadened the search to the distance Bingo could have traveled within that time. I didn't want to think about someone picking him up and taking him farther. Though I knew he loved me, he seldom met anyone who didn't merit a tail wag and a big slobbery kiss. He loved to go on car rides so much I had to stop him from going home with family and friends every time they visited.

By the time night fell, the reflection of the streetlight on the stark white paper I'd used for my posters hurt my eyes. The car keys rattled in my hands, aching from the cold. I knew I needed to get home before it was too dangerous to drive.

I had just gotten into my faded red Honda CR-V and buckled the seat belt when my cell phone rang. I automatically hit cancel when I didn't recognize the number. I cursed, realizing my cell was the number I'd posted on the posters. Just as I started to redial the caller, my phone rang again.

"Hello," I heard my voice, almost squeaking from the tightness in my throat.

"Hi, my name's Nicole," a woman's sweet alto voice answered. "We just found your dog."

"Where are you?" My heart sped up. I hit the accelerator and had to stomp the brakes fast to prevent myself from rear-ending the parked car in front of me. I pulled back, forced myself to breathe, to calm down and get the information I needed to get Bingo back.

Then we would curl up on the couch and sleep. I'd taken the day off and since it was Friday, I wouldn't have to report back until Monday.

Nicole was patient and kind. She must have realized how upset I was and offered to bring Bingo to me, but I told her I was in my car right then and I could be there just as soon as I got the address.

It took me a bit longer, though. Once I'd gotten the address and directions written on the back of one of the LOST DOG posters, the writing blurred. I turned my face away before my relieved tears smeared the writing and just took a few moments to calm down. I never cried before I lost my husband, but his death opened the floodgates. The VA shrink told me to allow myself time to grieve. Tears were a natural part of mourning. Unfortunately, friends and family weren't quite as understanding.

Traffic wasn't bad. It was past rush hour and most people were settled somewhere for their evening meal.

Nicole's house was a sprawling ranch, well lit by the porch lights and a rectangle of light where they'd left the glass storm door open. It was the kind of place I'd hoped for when my husband's tour was finally over and we could go back closer to family.

I rushed up the walkway, Bingo stood behind the glass at the front door, his mouth open in the typical golden grin and his tail wagging high on his back.

I stopped a few feet away, both relieved and annoyed. I'd been miserable and he'd clearly had a great time.

A couple appeared at the door. The woman, who seemed to be Nicole from the phone call, was small and brown-skinned with a golden Afro; she reached down and grabbed Bingo's collar before she opened the door. I caught the flash of her brilliant smile just as I reached the entrance and knelt opening my arms to Bingo as soon as the door was open. Nicole let go of his collar and he nearly knocked me over on the front walkway, covering my nose and mouth with sloppy doggy kisses.

"Come on in," Nicole's voice was even lovelier in person. "You must be tired from trying to find him."

Was that ever an understatement. At that moment, I could have just sunk down on their porch and slept. I wobbled when I tried to stand up and offered a grateful smile to her partner who extended a strong hand to help me up.

"Thank you for calling me," I said, looking up into the man's face for the first time. From the high angular cheekbones and bronze skin, I suspected he was Native American. Light from the room beyond reflected off shining raven hair with an occasional bolt of silver shot through. His broad-shouldered silhouette filled the doorway.

"This is my husband, Kevin," Nicole said in her low rich voice. "Bingo started following him on his run this afternoon."

I nodded and stuck out my hand to shake, returning their smiles. As my palm connected with Kevin's, I couldn't blame Bingo one bit. Looking at the handsome muscular man, even as tired as I was, I would follow his backside too.

"You must be exhausted," Kevin said. "Why don't you come in and rest before you drive back home?"

I nodded gratefully, hoping I didn't look as wasted as I felt.

"Can I get you something to eat or drink?" Nicole asked.

"No," I said, my voice coming out a tired rasp. I hadn't had much of either since Bingo was lost, but I just wanted to get home and rest.

I sank down into a well-cushioned blue leather sectional with the couple sitting companionably on either side of me. Bingo took a spot at our feet, looking up at me with his merry brown eyes. My head shook as my breath came freely for the first time since I'd seen the unlocked gate. I wanted to be angry at him, but how could I? A smile curved my lips, and I reached down to pet him.

"I need to write you a check," I said. Dread knotted my stomach. I had enough for Bingo's food, gas, and I'd see if I could bum a few meals off coworkers until payday. Worth every penny to get him back.

"No." Both of them said the word at once with no hesitation.

"Thank you."

"Hope it's okay," Nicole said. "Kevin went out and got him some dry food. It was what we fed our dog . . . We'll send the bag back with you, of course."

I nodded, noting Nicole's eyes drifting to a photo on the fireplace of the couple standing lovingly between an elegant-looking black and tan German shepherd.

"I'm sorry . . ." God I was so tired and so grateful they'd found my dog.

"Oh honey . . ." Nicole's voice softened and she scooted closer, wrapping her arms around me. Bingo rested his head on my knees and Kevin laid a large soothing hand on my shoulder. For the first time in months, I felt comfortable, safe, cared for.

They introduced themselves. Kevin was a professor of anthropology at UT and Nicole worked for one of the big-name companies that'd located to Austin recently. Looking around, I could almost sense their interests from the décor, a mix of Native artifacts, rocks, and modern art.

"Tell me about you . . ." Nicole said.

I generally didn't share my life with strangers, but Nicole was good at giving me her undivided and uncritical attention. Whenever I paused, she'd ask the perfect question to get me started talking again. Pretty soon, I was talking to her like I would to my oldest friends who were all too far away now. I told everything about our courtship, the places we were stationed, and my husband's death.

And then, I talked about how much I had missed him. I

never intended to continue living where we'd last been stationed before he was sent to A-stan, but I couldn't quite leave the place where we'd come with so many dreams.

"What about companionship? Sex?" Nicole asked.

I sighed.

Nicole glanced at Kevin, who nodded.

"We'd be glad to help you with that . . ."

I stared incredulously from one to the other. Both Kevin and Nicole offered themselves to me. I'd been curious about women since middle school, but I'd never found a female friend inclined to experiment. I turned my head and boldly kissed Nicole's full lips. Her tongue quickly parted my lips and thrust against mine. My hands roved from her delightfully rough kinky hair to her firm ass. For the first time in months, every nerve ending from the top of my head to the soles of my feet tingled with sensation.

"Come on," Kevin said. He stood, indicating a closed door that I took to be the bedroom. "Bingo will be fine out here . . ."

I took Kevin's extended hand and allowed him to pull me to my feet.

"After you," he murmured, gesturing to the door.

It'd been a long time since I had strutted my stuff, but I made sure my hips swayed with every step.

I paused in the threshold, my knees wobbling. Firelight from a modern-looking glass fireplace cast flickering illumination on the room. A king-size bed with a plush comforter beckoned me.

Nicole faced me, raised her arms, and pulled off her top, exposing warm bronze breasts with pert dark areoles. Her hands moved downward. The zipper of her jeans hissed softly. She let the softly faded denim fall to the floor, baring her body to the firelight. Nicole's golden hair haloed her head. But below the waist, she'd shaved her pubic hair into the shape of a heart and dyed it candy-apple red.

My breath caught. I swallowed hard to empty the sudden flood of moisture in my mouth.

I followed as Nicole backed to the bed. Bedcovers whispered seductively as she gracefully laid herself down, opening her legs.

My breath stuttered as I kicked off my shoes, then pulled off my sweater and jeans.

I plunged down on my knees between Nicole's spread legs. My trembling hand sought out her lower lips. I thrust my index finger inside the moist mouth of her vagina. Shuddering, I pressed my tongue to her throbbing clit.

I did to Nicole what I always wanted a man to do to me. My fingers slid in and out of her as I alternately stroked her clit and lower lips with my tongue. She gasped and thrust her hips against my mouth, asking for more.

My body shuddered as Nicole's back arched. She cried out and lay back against the pillows gasping.

"My turn." Kevin's deep voice sounded behind me as I felt strong warm hands take hold of my panties and pull them down around my knees.

I rolled on my back. My body was near white compared to his, but in typical redhead fashion, I flushed from my forehead down to my chest.

Damn! Kevin was impressive with his clothes off. My heart did a tap dance in my chest. He'd undone his hair and let it fall around his shoulders in a cascade of silver-shot black silk. A thunderbird tattoo was emblazoned across his broad chest.

"Oh my god," I stared at a tracery of crooked scars beneath his tattoo on his ribs and abdomen.

"You should have seen the other guy." Kevin's voice went low and rough.

My jaw dropped when I looked farther down. I ached for him, but I knew it'd be better for both of us if I gave him an appetizer.

I moved forward to sit at the edge of the bed and let my hands wander freely as I caressed his taut belly and firm buttocks with my hands, stroking and squeezing. Kevin gasped, thrusting toward my face.

"Here," Nicole passed me a tube of cherry-flavored lube. I squeezed out the lube and rubbed it between my hands to warm it. I slid my hands down the length of him, applying the delicious smelling lube salted with his own fragrance.

I swallowed several times before I let myself taste him. While I caressed the tip of his penis with my tongue, both my hands ranged along its length, twisting and moving in opposite directions.

Nicole moved closer, her breath coming faster as her hand glided down my side and between my legs.

A low moan escaped from my lips as Nicole's fingers entered me. My whole body shook.

Nicole guided me back on the bed to the pillows. She sat by my side as Kevin moved over me. He kissed me long and hard on the mouth, then his own lips shifted downward to my neck, my breasts.

He made it just to my bikini line before he retraced where he'd kissed before. He entered me just as he pressed his lips once again to my mouth.

I groaned against his mouth as my legs opened wider and my hips thrust up to welcome him.

Kevin read my body like a book. He took me just to the brink and stopped, cooling us both down with slower strokes and more kisses. Then, he'd shift back, moving faster, sending me into ecstasy.

When Kevin finally let me come, I felt him climaxing close behind.

I got the first decent night's sleep in months lying between the two of them that night with Bingo on the floor at our feet. We spent the weekend together, easing our mutual grief and enjoying one another's company.

We got together at least once a week for the next month. Both Kevin and Nicole made themselves available by phone or text should I need them.

Then I got the letter from my employer.

I showed up on their doorstep in tears, holding the letter.

Nicole, looking stricken, took it from my hands. Her eyes widened as she read.

"This is great news!" She handed the paper back to me. "Kevin, they're offering her a transfer and a promotion!"

"But I have to leave here." I barely choked the words out.

"Did you plan on staying here forever?" Kevin asked softly.

I shook my head, took a breath, and said, "But I'll be leaving the two of you."

"And you'll be going back closer to home, family, and friends." Kevin took the letter from Nicole and read the location. "Not like we won't have ways of staying in touch, and we can always come visit."

I nodded, feeling the knot in my chest abruptly lessening.

"And you will find people there," Nicole said. "Now that you know what you're looking for. . . ."

Kevin chuckled. "Just let Bingo help you pick them out."

BOB & CAROL
& TED (BUT
NOT ALICE)

M. Christian

"What are you afraid of?" Not spoken with scorn; with challenge though. This was Carol, after all. His Carol. The question was sweet, sincere, one lover to another: Really, honestly, what are you frightened of?

Robert fiddled with his glass of ice tea, gathering his thoughts. He trusted Carol—hell, he'd been happily married to her for five years so he'd better—but even so, it was a door he hadn't opened in a long time.

They were sitting in their living room. A gentle rain tapping at the big glass doors to the patio, dancing on the pale blue surface of the pool beyond. In the big stone fireplace, a gentle fire licked at the glowing embers of a log.

Carol smiled—and, as always, when she did Bob felt himself sort of melt, deep inside. Carol . . . it shocked him sometimes how much he loved her, trusted her, loved to simply be with her. He counted himself so fortunate to have found the other half of himself in the tall, slim, brown-haired woman. They laughed at the same jokes, they appreciated the same year of jazz, they both could eat endless platters of sashimi, and—in the bedroom, the garage, the kitchen, in the pool, in the car, and everywhere else the mood struck them. Their lovemaking was always delightful, often spectacular.

"I don't know," Bob finally said, taking a long sip of his drink (*needs more sugar,* he thought absently). "I mean I think about it sometimes. Not like I don't like what we do, but sometimes it crops up. A lot of the time it's hot, but other times it's kinda . . . fuck, disconcerting, you know? Like I should be thinking of what we're doing, what I want to do with you"—a sly smile, a hand on her thigh, kneading gently—"instead of thinking about, well, another guy."

Carol leaned forward, grazing her silken lips across his. As always, just that simple act—one sweeping kiss—made his body, especially his cock, stiff with desire. "Sweet," she said, whispering hoarsely into his ear, "I don't mind. I think it's hot. I really do."

Bob smiled, flexing his jean-clad thighs to relish his spontaneous stiffness. "I know. It just feels weird sometimes. I can't explain it."

"What do you think about? Talk to me about it. Maybe that'll help a little bit." Her hand landed in his lap, curled around his shaft. "Pretend I'm not here," she added, with a low laugh.

He responded with a matching chuckle. "Oh yeah, right," he said, leaning forward to meet her lips. They stayed together, lips on lips, tongues dancing in hot mouths. Bob didn't know how to respond, so he just followed his instincts—his hand drifted up to cup Carol's firm, large breasts. Five years and she still had the power to reach down into his sexual self, to get to him at a cock-and-balls level. But there was something else.

"I think it's hot," Carol said, breaking the kiss with a soft smack of moisture. "I think about it a lot, really. The thought of you with—what was his name again?"

Bob doubted Carol had really forgotten, but he smiled and played again. "Charley. College friend." Charley: brown curls, blue eyes, broad shoulders, football, basketball, geology, math, made a wicked margarita. Charley: late one night in their dorm room, both drunk on those wicked margaritas, Charley's hand on Bob's knee, then on his hard cock. "We fooled around for most of the semester, then his father died. Left him the business. We stayed in touch for a year or so, then, well, drifted away. You know."

"I think it's wonderful," Carol said, smiling, laughing, but also tender, caring, knowing there was a Charley-shaped hole somewhere deep inside Bob. Carefully, slowly, she inched down the zipper on his shorts until the tent of his underwear was clearly visible, a small dot of precome marking the so-hard tip of his cock. "I think about it when we play. When we fuck."

Bob suspected, but hearing Carol say it added extra iron to his already throbbing hard-on. Carol normally wasn't one to talk during sex. This new, rough voice was even more of a turn-on.

Bob felt a glow start, deep down. Even with Carol, Charley was something private—but hearing Carol's voice, he felt like he could, really, finally share it. "He was something else, Charley was. Big guy, never would have thought it to look at him. That sounds stupid, doesn't it?"

"No it doesn't. You're speaking from the heart, sexy. Since when is anyone's heart logical or fair?" Carol had gotten his shorts down, quickly followed by his underwear. Bob's cock had never seemed so big or so hard in his life. It was like two parts of his life had met, with the force of both working to make him hard . . . so damned hard. Carol kissed the tip, carefully savoring the bead of come just starting to form again at the tip.

He smiled down at her, taking a moment to playfully ruffle her hair before allowing himself to melt down into the sofa. "I wouldn't call him 'sweet' or 'nice,' but he could be sometimes. He just liked . . . fuck . . ." The words slipped from his mind as Carol opened her mouth and, at first—slowly, carefully— started to suck on his cock. "Fuck . . . yeah, he liked life, I guess. I don't even think he thought of himself as gay or anything. He just liked to fuck, to suck, to get laid, you know. But it was special. I can't really explain it."

"You loved him, didn't you—at least a little bit?" Carol said, taking her lips off his cock for a moment to speak. As she did, she stroked him, each word a downward or upward stroke.

Bob didn't say anything. He just leaned back and closed his eyes. He knew she was right but that was one thing he wasn't quite willing to say—not yet. He'd come a long way, but that was still in the distance.

Carol smiled, sweetly, hotly, and dropped her mouth onto his cock again. This time her sucking, licking, stroking of his cock was faster, more earnest, and Bob could tell that she was aching to fuck, to climb on top of him and ride herself to a shattering, glorious orgasm. But she didn't. Instead, she kept sucking, kept stroking his cock, occasionally breaking to whisper, then say in a raw, hungry voice: "I think it's hot . . . not him just sucking your cock . . . but that you have had that. Bet sometimes . . . we look at the same guy . . . and want to know what he'd be like . . . to suck . . . to fuck."

Even though Bob was . . . somewhere else, damned near where Carol wanted to be, he knew she was right. It was hot, it was special, and he recognized that. He wanted to haul her off her knees, get dressed, and bolt out the door to do just that. The kid who bagged their groceries sometimes at the Piggly Wiggly, that one linebacker, Russell Crowe—he wanted to take them home, take off their shirts, lick their nipples, suck their cocks, suck their cocks, suck their cocks—

Then something went wrong. Just on the edge of orgasm, Carol stopped. Bob felt slapped, like ice water had just been dumped into his lap. He opened his eyes and looked, goggle-eyed, as Carol got up off the floor, straightening her T-shirt over very hard nipples. "Didn't you hear that? Of all times for someone to ring the fucking doorbell."

Tugging up his pants, Bob rehearsed what he'd say: Mormons? Slam the door in their faces. Door-to-door salesman? The same. Someone needing directions? "Sorry, but you're *way* off," then do the same. . . .

Just as Bob got to the living room door, he heard Carol, who'd been a lot more dressed to start with, saying, "Ted! How's it hanging?"

Bob rounded the corner, a smile already spreading across his face. Of all the people to have knocked on their front door, Ted was probably the only one who would have understood.

Ted and his charming wife Alice lived just across town. Normally, Bob and Carol would never in a million years have crossed paths with them, but it so happened that Ted worked in the coffee place right across the street from where Bob worked. After six months of going back and forth, Bob finally struck up a conversation with Ted and found out, much to his delight, that the tall, sandy-haired young man and he had a lot in common: the Denver Broncos, weekend sailing, and Russell Crowe movies. Bob and Carol felt very relaxed and even sometimes sexually playful around Ted and Alice—even going so far as to having a kind of sex party one night, when they all got way too wasted on tequila and some primo green bud that Ted had scored the night before. All they'd done was watch each other fuck, but it had been more than enough to blast Bob and Carol into happy voyeuristic bliss and fuel their erotic fantasies for weeks afterward.

"Low and to the right," Ted answered, smiling wide and broad and planting a quick kiss on Carol's cheek. Bob gave Ted his own quick greeting—a full-body hug that only until he finished did Bob realize had probably given Ted more than he expected with regard to Bob's still rock-hard dick.

Bob and Carol smiled at each other, feeling relaxed and still playful in the presence of their friend. "Where's Alice at, Teddy? Somewhere in the depths of Columbia?" Bob asked. Alice was the other half of Bean Seeing You, their little coffee house, and was often away trying to wrangle up all kinds of stimulating delicacies, not all of them coffee-related.

"Worse than that," Ted said, playfully ruffling his friend's brown locks. "Deepest, darkest Bakersfield. I'm kinda worried about her—the last expedition down there vanished without a trace."

Everyone laughing, more out of released tension than Ted's weird brand of humor, they retreated back to the living room and the couch. As Bob and Ted sprawled out on the couch while Carol got some drinks, Bob couldn't help but wonder if their friend had figured out that they'd been almost screwing their brains out a few minutes before. The thought of it made Bob grin wildly.

"Come on, bro," Ted said, picking up on the smile. "Out with it."

Suddenly tongue-tied, Bob was glad when Carol walked in with three tall, cool drinks. "One for the man of the house"— Bob—"one for the handsome stranger"—Ted—"and one for the horny housewife"—Carol. "Cheers!" she concluded, taking a hefty swallow of her own drink.

Bob and Ted toasted her, Bob almost coughing as he drank—
the drinks were stiff and then some. He smiled to himself again
as he sank back into the sofa. Talking about Charley made him
feel like a secret had been released from some dark, compressed
part of his mind. He felt light, airy, almost like he was hovering
over his body, looking down at Ted—tall, curly haired, quick
and bright Ted—and Carol. Carol, who even just thinking of
made his body and mind recall their wonderful lovemaking.

Sneaking a furtive glance at Ted, Bob looked his friend over
more carefully. In his new, unburdened vision, Ted looked . . .
well, he wasn't like Charley, but there was still something about
Ted that made Bob think of his college friend—no, his college
lover. Something about their height, their insatiable appetite for
life, their humor.

"Is it hot in here or is it just me?" Carol piped up, laughing
at her own cliché. Bob and Ted laughed, too, but then the sound
dropped away to a compressed silence as Carol lifted off her
T-shirt and theatrically mopped her brow.

Bob's mind bounced from Carol's beautiful breasts, and her
obviously very erect nipples, to Ted's rapt attention on them. He
was proud of Carol, proud that she was so lovely, so sexy. He
wanted to reach out and grab her, pull her to him. He wanted to
kiss her nipples as Ted watched. He wanted to sit her down on
the couch, spread her strong thighs and lick her cunt until she
screamed, moaned, and held on to Bob's hair as orgasm after
orgasm rocketed through her, while Ted watched. He wanted
to bend her over, slide his painfully hard cock into her, and
then fuck her till she moaned and bucked against him as Ted
watched. He wanted Ted . . .

Carol's shorts came off next. Naked, she stood in front of
them. Like a goddess, she rocked, back and forth, showing off
her voluptuous form. But even though he loved her and thought

she was probably the most beautiful woman he'd ever seen, Bob turned to look at Ted.

Ted, with the beautiful Carol standing right there in the room in front of him was, instead, looking at Bob.

Bob felt his face grow flushed with . . . no, not with what he expected. It wasn't embarrassment. Dimly, he was aware of Carol walking toward him, getting down on her hands and knees again, and in a direct repeat of only minutes before, playfully tugging his cock out of his shorts and starting to suck on it.

Still watching Ted watching him—and Carol sucking his cock—Bob smiled at him. In Carol's mouth, his cock jumped with a sudden influx of pure lust.

Carol, breaking her hungry relishing of his dick, said, "Bob, I really think Ted would like you to suck his cock."

Now Bob was embarrassed, but not enough to keep him from silently nodding agreement.

"I'd love that," Ted said, his voice low and rumbling. "I really would."

"Take your pants off, Ted," Carol said, stroking Bob's cock. "I want to watch."

Ted did, quickly shucking his shirt as well as his threadbare jeans. He stood for a moment, letting Carol and Bob look at him. Bob had seen his friend's cock before, but for the first time he really looked at it. Ted was tall and thin, his chest bare and smooth. His cock was big, though maybe not as big as Bob's (a secret little smirk at that), but handsome. It wasn't soft, but it also wasn't completely hard. As Carol and Bob watched, Ted's cock grew firmer, harder, larger, until it stuck out from his lean frame at an urgent forty-five-degree angle.

"Bob . . ." Carol said, her voice purring with lust, " . . . suck Ted's cock. Please, suck it."

Ted crawled up on the sofa, lying down so that his head was on one armrest, his cock sticking straight up. His eyes were half closed, and a sweet, sexy, smile played on his lips.

Bob reached down, turning just enough to reach his friend and not dislodge Carol from her earnest sucking of his own dick, and gently took hold of Ted's cock. It was warm, almost hot, and slightly slick with a fine sheen of sweat. He could have looked at it for hours, days, but with Carol working hard on his own dick, he felt his pulse racing, his own hunger beating hard in his heart.

At first he just kissed it, tasting salty precome. With a flash of worry that he wouldn't be good, first he licked the tip, exploring the shape of the head with his lips and then his tongue. As his heart hammered more heavily and his own cock pulsed with sensation, he finally took the head into his mouth and gently sucked and licked. Ted, bless him, gave wonderful feedback, gently moaning and bucking his slim hips just enough to let Bob know that he was doing a good job.

As Carol worked him, he worked Ted. They were a long train of pleasure, a circuit of moans and sighs. Time seemed to stretch, and distance compressed until the whole world was just Ted's dick in Bob's mouth, Bob's dick in Carol's mouth—all on that wonderful afternoon.

Then, before he was even aware it was happening, Bob felt his orgasm pushing, heavy and wonderfully leaden, down through his body, down through his balls, down through his cock in a spasming release that made him break his earnest sucking of Ted's cock to moan, sigh, almost scream with pleasure. Smiling at his friend, Ted followed quickly behind, with only a few more jerks of his cock as Bob rested his head on Ted's knee.

Bob felt . . . good, like something important, magical, and special had happened. The world had grown, by just a little bit, but in a very special way. Resting on his friend's knee, Carol kissing his belly, he smiled. Everything all right with the world.

Later, the sun having set, and everyone being very much exhausted by many more hours of play, Ted stumbled to the front door, with Carol helping him navigate through the dim house. "Thanks for coming," she said with a sweet coo, almost a whisper, so as not to wake the heavily slumbering Bob in the next room. She kissed him, soft and sweet, smiling to herself at the variety of tastes on his lips.

"I was happy to. Very. Thanks for asking me to . . . come," Ted said, smiling, as he opened the front door.

Carol smiled. "Thank you for giving him such a wonderful gift. Next weekend then?"

"Definitely. Next time I'll bring Alice."

Another gentle kiss, a mutual "Good night," and the door was closed.

HOMECOMING

Teresa Noelle Roberts

I'm coming home.

Ethan and I had each received that text from Josh two days ago. We'd responded immediately, trying to coax out more information. We'd gotten a date and general time—tonight around nine—but nothing more, not even whether he was flying in or driving or slipping through a crack in the time-space continuum.

More importantly we knew nothing about why he was coming back to Boston. To us, the partners he hadn't broken up with when he moved on.

Josh had seemed happy in Nashville with Della, the genially crazy rockabilly singer who'd tempted him to follow when her career took her south. At least he'd acted like he was. A couple of months ago, we stopped hearing from him regularly, but we'd figured he was deep in the throes of a new book. When we'd lived together, he could go for days, sometimes weeks, barely speaking when the writing was going well. It was Josh's version of normal, and we'd figured silence was more of the same.

Obviously, we'd been wrong.

So on this cold, rainy night we waited for him to arrive. For answers to all the questions. For our boy to come home, whatever that meant.

When the doorbell rang, though, I checked the security camera. Our neighborhood was quiet, but it was still the outskirts of a big city. Besides, Josh wouldn't need the bell; he had a key.

He wasn't using it. Through the camera's fuzzy gaze, Josh was pale under the porch light, and his dark hair was plastered against his scalp by the rain. He was shivering. His denim jacket was too light for the weather, even dry, and at this point you could wring it out and end a drought. He carried only a backpack, big enough to hold a laptop but small enough to fit under the seat on a plane. It didn't look large enough for a man who'd said he was coming home, but Josh had always traveled light.

He waved at where he knew the camera was and tried to smile.

Josh had the most beautiful smile of anyone I'd ever known, but this one looked broken. Not as if he was forcing it for our benefit this one time when he was too tired to do it properly, but as if he'd forgotten how a smile worked.

Seeing that expression, I couldn't wonder why he hadn't used his key. He needed one of us to open the door and reassure him he was still welcome here.

We ran to the door. I fumbled at the locks, my hands shaking, almost too clumsy to cooperate. Ethan reached around me and finished the job.

For an uncomfortable second, we were all silent, frozen in place. Ethan recovered first. "It's about time you got here," he muttered in a way both Josh and I knew wasn't really grumpy, and opened his arms.

Josh stepped inside and closed the door behind him as if this were the most ordinary night of our lives. "I know." He'd picked up a hint of an accent in his year in Nashville; he'd started catching that drawl from Della, though, before he left Boston. "It was a longer walk than I remembered."

I finally found my voice. I wasn't thrilled that it came out so high and anxious, and even less thrilled that my first words were a dumb question but I'd managed to string words together, so it was a start. "You walked from the T station in this weather, you dork?"

Josh shrugged damply. "I've done it a million times. Not far enough to bother with an Uber and I didn't want to call you or Ethan . . ."

His voice trailed off. His dark eyes skipped away, looking at his soggy shoes instead of at us. It wasn't quick enough to hide what he wasn't saying. *In case it was too much trouble. In case you didn't really want to see me. In case it was beyond the terms of my welcome.* Desperately insecure on one level, yet bold enough to walk over a mile through sleet to a place he wasn't sure he belonged anymore.

"Silly boy. Of course we'd pick you up at the station. Or the airport. Or in Nashville if you'd needed us to."

Our silly boy, I wanted to say, but I didn't dare. He'd never been our sub or boy in the BDSM sense. The three of us had dabbled in kink, but not seriously enough to use that terminology. But he'd been ours, and we'd been his.

I couldn't ask if that was still true. Instead I added, "We never stopped loving you. We just stopped living with you."

"And fucking you," Ethan, ever the pragmatist, added. "But that was because you were too far away, and a little bit because poly or not, Della always looked like she wanted to cut anyone who got too close to you."

Josh laughed, an awkward chuckle washed in unshed tears. "Ethan, Abby . . . I'm sorry for the drama but it's all been so crazy."

"We understand," I murmured, though I for one wasn't sure I did. I opened my arms just before Ethan did, so when Josh came to me, Ethan wrapped his long, lanky self around both of us. Within seconds I'd sucked up enough rainwater from Josh that I should have been shivering.

Instead, I felt Josh warm in my heart.

I didn't know why he was here yet, or how long he'd be staying. But his presence was enough to thaw a part of me that I'd put on ice when he left.

I started tearing up and didn't try to fight it.

"You should get out of those wet clothes," Ethan finally murmured. His voice sounded thick, choked up as if he'd wanted to cry as blatantly as I was but couldn't let himself.

He paused as if he'd just realized what he'd said, and drew back just a little from the group hug. "As in you need to get warm, not as in let's get naked and engage in adult shenanigans." He barked out something between a chuckle and a cough. "Necessarily, that is. I mean, I've missed naked consenting-adult activity with you but you just walked in the door after being away a long time and . . . Fuck, I give up. There is no way this isn't going to sound awkward."

"Hot shower first," Josh said. "After that, I love the idea of consenting-adult-type activities, but I warn you I might just pass out. It's been a long day and I had to fly from Nashville via Chicago." He must have remembered how to smile, because his shy grin lit up the room.

"In that case," I said before I could even think about it,

"should we join you in the shower as lifeguards or something?"

"Please," was all Josh said, but in that word I caught an echo of what I'd wanted to say but hadn't dared: *My skin is hungry for yours.*

The kiss that followed was tentative and promising as a warm March day in Massachusetts. Not much tongue. No mindless, searing passion. But love and apologies and forgiveness and what I can only describe as mutual surrender.

When we moved apart, Ethan and Josh stared at each other. They hadn't kissed much, back in the day. Both of them thought of themselves as more straight than not and had been surprised by falling for each other. As far as I'd been able to figure out from their man-speak, fucking and sucking and mild kink had been fine, as had working together to make me limp with pleasure, but kissing seemed like a bridge too far.

You wouldn't think that from the kiss they shared now, standing in the foyer while the door fogged over from damp. They both looked surprised when it ended—but not embarrassed, and definitely turned on. "Well now." Ethan's voice was husky. "How about that shower?"

Josh went into the bathroom alone to pee. When he opened the door again, he was shirtless. He was thinner than he used to be, drawn and tired, but luminous, as if his soul was glowing through his skin. "I've missed you both."

"Me too." Ethan and I spoke almost simultaneously.

Josh reached for the zipper of jeans that must be icy cold and irritating. Then he stopped. "Is this really all right? Are you both sure?"

"Taking your jeans off is not all right," Ethan said, his voice harsh. "I want to do it for you." He knelt down in front of Josh, wrapped his arms around Josh's slim hips, and rested against his bare belly. His skin looked more coppery-brown than usual against Josh's pallor.

I enjoyed the view for a second. Then I walked behind Josh and started kissing his shoulder and neck. He shuddered.

I heard the snick as Ethan began to unzip Josh's jeans. A snick and a moan, and I wasn't sure which one of us was moaning. Maybe we all were. I wasn't sure where I stopped and the guys started, so I could have been making noise and not known it.

It took both of us, with help from Josh, to work the jeans off. Wet denim is nasty stuff with a mind of its own. But finally he was naked and we were both touching him, kissing him, stroking him, drinking in his skin, his scent. He smelled a little different than I remembered—stress, or a different diet, or maybe just the residue of a long trip—but it was still *him*. Our bed had held that warm spice smell for weeks after he left, even with clean sheets. I wanted to tell him that. Wanted to tell him everything. But that would have meant I had to stop kissing and licking.

His cock was getting harder by the second, though we hadn't touched it yet. Ethan's penis jutted against his tortured pants, and I was as wet as Josh had been when he came to our door. Josh clutched at us as if afraid we'd slip away. His kisses were almost bites. Unlike us, he was letting his hands brush over the outline of Ethan's cock, cup my pussy through my leggings. We were catching fire, but I could still feel Josh's goose bumps under my questing hands. I made myself say, "Shower. Warm shower."

Josh sounded half-drunk as he said, "That means you'll finally get naked too? About time."

We'd undressed Josh with some ceremony. We took off our own clothes as if they were burning us.

The water was hot, but Josh began to shake as it hit his skin. I wrapped myself around him and Ethan wrapped himself around both of us and we held on until the shaking passed, until we were all centered.

Despite all the emotions thick in the air, both men were harder than ever. The water had washed away some of my slick-ness, but juices still flowed from me, and my nipples were so sensitive that the water striking them was a tingly caress.

Josh was here. Naked. With us.

Everything might not be *all right* in a big-picture sense, but in the moment, it was damn near perfect. There was only one thing I could think of that would make it better.

One hand on Ethan for balance, I sank to my knees. "May I?" Once upon a time, we'd read each other's bodies so well that explicit verbal consent seemed necessary only if we were experimenting with some unfamiliar bit of kink. Tonight, we were new again, raw. Scared, or at least I was. It felt important to ask.

"I should be the one . . . I left. I fucked up. I should be on my knees, not you."

I snorted. "You'll get your turn, but not because you fucked up, which I'm not sure you did. I'm down here because I want to be. Because I love you—*we* love you." I was getting choked up, so I quickly added, "And because oral sex is fun whether you're giving or receiving, so we should all get to do both. But mostly because we love you."

Josh's face lit up again. "Please," he said. The one word contained so much I couldn't begin to unpack it.

Kneeling in a shower isn't precisely comfortable, even when you have two hot lovers in the shower with you and you're crazy with desire.

The discomfort felt right. Josh wasn't the only one with fucked-up ideas about penance, making amends. He'd gone with Della, but we'd let him go. Once we did, we hadn't done enough to keep in touch, to let him know we still loved him. Hadn't visited him in Nashville more than once.

I couldn't take back the lost time, couldn't even make up for it. But I could seize the moment we had now.

I took him into my mouth. I hadn't forgotten how he felt or tasted, but he was even more delicious than I'd remembered, fit better in my mouth. The shower's relentless rain stripped away the light smell of grimy Boston rain, but I caught hints of warm spice and musk. It wasn't a soap or cologne, simply Josh, and a host of sensual memories flooded back, other times I'd smelled and tasted him. He groaned and so did I, as best I could around that familiar yet once again new thickness.

Ethan, at first, kept one hand on my shoulder and one at the small of Josh's back. I wasn't sure if it was to give us a little time to play without him or because he wasn't sure where to touch first. This night felt miraculous and perilous at the same time and that might shake even his confidence.

Before long, though, his right hand stroked its way to my breasts. Weighed and squeezed each as he caressed and pinched its nipple, sending zings of pleasure through my body to meet up with the ones swirling in me from touching Josh, sucking Josh. I forced my eyes open through the weight of bliss to see Ethan's other hand was playing with Josh's butt. From my viewpoint I couldn't tell if he was teasing the asshole or maybe just stroking the skin, but he definitely engaged with Josh's gorgeous backside in some way.

Josh was groaning, and Ethan was crooning "Oh yes," and making it sound much richer and dirtier than those two words had any right to do. My body ached with need—not just the obvious lips and nipples and pussy, but even the palms of my hands and the soft skin of my belly.

Abruptly Josh blurted, "Too fast!" and pulled back. His

eyes, when I looked up, were wild. "Don't want to come yet. Take our time . . ." The man was a writer and editor, but at the moment English grammar was clearly beyond him.

Not that I'd do better. I wasn't even going to try to speak because I knew I wouldn't make any sense.

"We'll run out of hot water soon anyway." Ethan managed a complete sentence, but it sounded like it took work.

I nodded. I could nod, even lost in lust as I was.

The bedroom would be more comfortable anyway.

Huge bed. Warmth. And a nice thick carpet for the moment when Josh asked for his turn on his knees.

Which was as soon as we all got into the bedroom.

I'd been greedy, giving all my oral attentions to one person. Josh alternated between sucking Ethan and licking my clit. His hot tongue on my most sensitive spot was a tease, not the obsessive focus I'd lavished on him, but I couldn't complain. Not when I got to watch him swallow Ethan's length, or swirl his tongue around the swollen head, when it wasn't my turn for mind-numbing bliss.

"Been too long," I whispered. That covered so many things, but one of them was watching Ethan be pleasured by another man. In the past year, we'd been reminded it was hard enough to meet someone one of us liked and lusted after and the other could tolerate as an occasional dinner guest, let alone that we both wanted to get naked with. There'd been a distinct lack of moments like this.

Not that they would have been the same with a different third person. Fun, but not the same. Josh was . . . Josh. It was magical to play voyeur with two people I loved as well as desired. To enjoy not just their physical appeal, but the way I felt included—almost felt their hands and lips on me—even when we weren't touching.

Between the visual pleasure and the more visceral one of Josh's tongue swirling on my clit, the soft, welcome scratch of his beard on my skin, I ramped up quickly, soaring toward orgasm. There was no physical reason to hold back; I was one of the lucky women who could keep going like an Energizer Bunny. But this night I craved that tension, wanting to feel what Josh felt, what I suspected Ethan would choose to feel. The ache of desire, the throb of need, swirled in a pleasantly open place that might have filled with the ache and throb of missing Josh in our lives.

But Josh was back. We still weren't sure why he'd returned or whether he'd stay but for now he was here, with us.

For a fraction of a second, I let myself worry about the future. Then Ethan pointed to the bed and told Josh, "Lie down. I want to be comfortable while I'm sucking you." The worry fled, along with any thoughts of anything other than pleasure.

Josh in Ethan's mouth—good lord, that was a beautiful sight. I watched the slow slide of Ethan's lips along Josh's length, the small shudder of Josh's abs, and felt a sense of rightness I hadn't in a long time. Once I wrapped my own lips around Ethan's cock, I couldn't enjoy that glorious view, but it didn't matter. I heard. I felt. I tasted.

Ethan shifted position a little so he could lick me.

It was awkward . . . and yet it was perfect. Perfectly awkward. Awkwardly perfect. That kind of circle reads better in fiction than it plays out in real life. Too much going on. I couldn't decide whether to focus on the giving, the receiving, or the sounds and smells and touches that formed the big picture. Aroused as I was, it was simultaneously too much and too little to push me over the edge. I'd bet it was the same for the guys. Yet being part of that circle of pleasure with my two beloveds was about as good as life gets.

Until I had an even better idea. It took me a bit to find enough words to articulate it, and longer to pull my mouth away from Ethan's cock. But I finally managed to push out the words, "Three-way fuck?"

It wasn't exactly poetry, but it got the point across. There was a little more talking to work out details and logistics, using sign language when the connection between brains and mouths refused to cooperate.

"Abby should be the sandwich filling, since it was her idea," Josh proposed.

I'd always been game to take one of the men in my pussy and the other in my ass. Not much beat that incredible fullness, or that sense of being overpowered by pleasure and muscle while being in control and completely surrounded by and filled with love.

Because it *was* so incredible—and especially because of the "surrounded by and filled with love" angle, I had another thought for tonight. And as I said it, Ethan echoed me. "No, Josh. You should be."

His eyes widened, and his mouth opened slackly. At first, I thought he was going to say no, out of misplaced guilt, or because he was overwhelmed and couldn't handle it, or maybe just wasn't in the mood for someone in his ass tonight. Then the slack mouth morphed into a beaming, bemused smile. "God, yes," he breathed, not an exclamation but a prayer.

I don't remember anyone actually reaching for lube and condoms, but somehow, they appeared. Ethan and I discovered it didn't work well for two excited people to roll a condom onto a third person's cock. It was, however, fun to try, for us as much as for Josh. In the end, though, Josh said, "I'll sheath the beast myself," and we all laughed so hard that tears threatened. None of us remembered who'd come up with that particular ridiculous phrase for "putting on a condom" but it was part of our shared story.

So much a part of the three of us that neither Ethan nor I used it after Josh left.

Applying lube, on the other hand, worked as group foreplay. Stroking it along hard cocks. Sinking it into Josh's ass. He was tight around even my slender finger at first, but he made the most gratifying noise and pushed back eagerly. Soon, he was more than ready to welcome Ethan's thicker digits.

I was slick, juices glistening on my thighs. But Ethan and Josh still worked together to lube me up, ass as well as cunt. In a quick and dirty negotiation, I'd said I'd prefer Josh in my cunt tonight and both men were fine with that, but apparently they liked the noises I made when one of them played with my pussy and the other one slid a greased finger into my ass. Faced with that dual stimulation, I gave up my earlier resolve to hold off and let orgasm roll over me like a happy tidal wave.

Our ultimate destination was temporarily forgotten in the pleasures of the moment, of clever hands, questing lips, and two hard cocks and my wet pussy teasing against sensitive flesh. But eventually we ended up as we'd planned.

Me on my back, legs wide. Josh deep inside me, butt high. Ethan slowly, patiently, entering Josh's ass.

Josh held himself still as Ethan entered him. Josh was shaking, his face strained. Ecstasy, mostly, though I knew from my own experience that there'd be some burning discomfort that would stand out from the pleasure before swirling into it. A little of the strain remained, though, after Ethan was as deep inside him as Josh was inside me and I wrapped my legs, as best I could, around them both. Through gritted teeth, Josh said, "Not going to last long."

"Don't need to." I kissed him before going on. "I'm going to come again any second." Josh visibly relaxed.

"And your ass feels so sweet . . . No, *you* feel so sweet. You both do." Ethan never finished the thought, which was obviously heading toward a declaration that he'd come quickly too. Instead, he started to stroke slowly in and out. Josh picked up his rhythm and transferred it to me.

It had been a long time since we'd fucked like this. If I'd thought more about it, I'd have predicted it would be ungainly, though still hot. But we read each other's cues just right. Picked up the pace just when the slowness became too much to bear, held back when someone needed a lighter touch. Erotic perfection, if there can be such a thing. Messy, sweaty erotic perfection, slippery with lube, broken with laughter and sobs, and for me, breathless because I was half-crushed by the weight of two good-sized men. The messiness made it better.

Perfection can't last long. I was looking at Josh's transfigured face, at Ethan's intent one, feeling the doubled thrust— Josh into me, Ethan into Josh and through him, into me as well. Josh felt and moved like the man I remembered and at the same time like someone new, slimmer and more intense. It was all too much. I closed my eyes, saw a supernova, opened them again to my men's beautiful, strained faces. The supernova spread throughout my body and I cried out and convulsed around Josh. Around both of them, though only one was literally in my cunt. Josh froze in mid-stroke and roared out his own orgasm. Ethan, as usual, came almost silently, a few wild thrusts and a huffed "Yes."

"Don't leave again," I whispered against Josh's chest once we'd curled into our sticky post-coital puppy pile.

He kissed the top of my head, then stretched to kiss Ethan, who was curled around him. "I can't promise that. I need to sort some things out in Nashville. But I promise I'll always come back."

That was good enough for now, sated and sleepy as we were.

We didn't press the issue in the morning over coffee and bagels. Josh arrived at it by a circuitous route, announcing out of nowhere, "Della's doing well in Nashville. Performing almost every night. But . . ."

His words trailed off. Ethan filled in. "She wanted you out with her every night, didn't she?" Josh did his best writing at night; what he saw of the daytime was for his freelance editing, sex, and sleep. We made it work with our own crazy schedules but we'd had to plan evenings out as a triad carefully, with plenty of advance warning.

Josh nodded. "I tried. But I couldn't go out as much as she wanted me to and keep up with my own work. I hated the crowds and the noise and all the drunk, stoned strangers I had to make nice with for Della's sake." I shuddered for him, knowing what an introvert he was. "And being around all those people I didn't give a fuck about made me miss you two more, which didn't help. So I stopped going and started drinking too much at home alone. I missed a book deadline because I was writing absolute crap when I could write at all. I missed you two. I missed the me I was when I lived in Boston. I missed Della because we hardly saw each other anymore. After a while, she started staying out all night sometimes, coming home after I'd crashed. That would have been all right if she'd told me she had a date or whatever. I wouldn't have a problem with her seeing someone on the side, but I hate being kept in the dark. We kept pretending everything was fine, though. Maybe after the big, dramatic decision to move to Nashville together, we couldn't admit we might have made a mistake. We put off talking about our problems for so

long that once we let ourselves get into it, it turned into the kind
of fight that changes things. Ends things or at least reshapes
them—we're still not sure which. I do love her, even though I'm
angry about the secrets. I think she still loves me. But we can't
live together. If she and I get back together, it'll have to be as
something totally different and we have no idea what. So I came
here. I didn't know where else to go. But I knew you'd let me
stay while I got my shit together."

It was a long speech for him—Josh was better at the written
word—and there were plenty of gaps in the story. But it was a
start.

I reached across the small kitchen table and hugged him.
"You can stay here as long as you want or need to." *You can
stay forever*, I thought, but didn't say. I wasn't sure if it was too
soon or just already understood.

"It's your home," Ethan added. "It's always been your
home."

"No," he said, "you two are my home. I can visit other
places, other people, but you two are home. And it turns out
I'm a homebody."

I was the first to start crying, but before I could do more than
sniffle once, we all were. Even Ethan, who claimed he couldn't
weep from sorrow, learned he could tear up from joy.

Josh was home. We still had a lot to work out, the three of us
and Della, but I had faith we'd do it right this time.

SNAKEFRUIT

Anne Tourney

Octavia sits at the kitchen table, spooning peanut butter from a jar. Her husband's cat tiptoes toward the litter box. Octavia growls; the tabby retreats. To the cat, Octavia must look like a devourer of felines—her belly huge, her teeth gleaming—but the thought pleases her. Her pregnancy has been full of epiphanies, ranging from the comic to the frightful. Nausea, bizarre forms of water storage, the endless exposure of her vulva to doctors and nurses. She's spent a lifetime with her heels in stirrups.

Her husband Reggie lives in awed expectation. Out of reverence and terror, he has stopped making love to her. Most of the time Octavia doesn't mind. Since her pregnancy, she enjoys solo sex more than ever. Alone in the afternoons, she explores pleasure like an unfamiliar neighborhood—a shabby, wild neighborhood. When she comes, a new pulse thunders in her groin, and her tiny conspirator rollicks inside her. Reggie reads his mother's yellowed copy of *Doctor Spock* and adjusts the budget. Octavia masturbates.

Closing the peanut butter jar, she pushes herself away from the table. She hasn't worked on her thesis or written a line of poetry since her first trimester; she's diverted her creativity into a search for food. The quest begins in the morning, after Reggie's farewell kiss, and ends after midnight. Two monstrous, dueling appetites—for food and sex—propel her through the day. No desire to read or write. She never even picks up a pen anymore, except when she writes out a check at the grocery store, which she raids several times a week. The cashiers, middle-aged women, smile sympathetically. The teenage stock boys blush at her fecundity. Pushing her cart through the parking lot, Octavia chomps pretzels or pickled okra. The Madonna's privilege is a serene ignorance of appearances.

Octavia had expected to finish her doctorate, publish a book of poetry, coast comfortably from literary to maternal fulfill-ment. She and Reggie would enjoy a few self-indulgent years before facing the stark engagement of parenthood. And as they came to know each other deeply, their love would sink taproots into the mulch of their prosperity. Everything changed.

They've been married for eight months when Octavia discovers Reggie's secret. She's furrowing through the storage closet, looking for her wedding album, when she finds a box of magazines. *Playboy, Penthouse.* Some slightly spicier publi-cations: lots of tumescent members on the verge of plunging into prim holes. Then, at the very bottom, scenes from a land without limits. Creamy fleurs-de-lis spout triumphantly over breasts and lips and buttocks. Tongues prod labia of all flavors. Lips vacuum yards and yards of purple prick. Stupefied, Octavia falls to her knees. Pages full of flesh slide shimmering out of her hands. It numbs her, this universe of multicolored tissue, with its constellations of nipples and its glistening cuntscapes. Forests of fur and fingers. Endless eruptions of ejaculate. Go

West, young man, to a frontier where the cock never softens and the cunt never runs dry!

Octavia stares at the pictures. Of course she has seen pornographic images before, but never in such abundance. The most obscene publications have no copy at all. Words detract from the brute immanence of flesh. At first she wants to destroy the magazines. She wants to rip the pages apart and pin them on the walls, to relish Reggie's shame when he sees his home adorned with cunts and pricks. Or she could pile them in the litter box and set them on fire; flame was more appropriate. She would pour cognac over them and make her husband light the match. Reggie's auto-da-fé.

But she's tired, too tired. Why douse obscenity with violence? Eventually they will talk, quietly and maturely, about Reggie's collection. They will communicate. And Reggie, his head lowered in remorse, will shuffle out to the incinerator to throw the offensive material away.

It's not that Octavia objects to Reggie admiring other women, or even lusting after them—quite the contrary. From the beginning of their marriage, she and Reggie decided that they would leave their relationship open to other individuals, of either sex, who might become friends or lovers. But the routines of marriage, the politics of academia, and now the demands of pregnancy have eclipsed their polyamorous visions. How could she or Reggie search for new lovers, Octavia has wondered, when they've both been blinded by the glare of adult reality?

In all honesty, Octavia is not disappointed with Reggie's exploration of his own sexuality, but with the vulgar mediocrity of his choice of erotic outlets. The kind of porn he's chosen is so . . . predictable. So depressingly mundane. She would rather have him taking a flesh-and-blood lover to his bed; at least that would imply that he had a heart as well as a libido.

Wearily Octavia dumps the magazines into the box. Poor Reggie. His sex drive is high, and he knows a trick or two, but he's never knocked her world out of orbit. When they have sex (when they *used* to have sex) his mind probably teems with the purple iconography of porn.

Well, why not? In her hottest moments, Octavia used to imagine the bass guitarist she fucked after her college graduation party. Unfortunately, that guitarist disappeared from her life long ago, along with the lusty echoes of his electric guitar.

Like Bluebeard's bride, Octavia can't stop thinking about her husband's Secret. She has endowed it with a capital S; it gives the noun a lewd Victorian majesty. *My Secret*, by Sir R—. She hovers around the coat closet where the box sits, and her hands itch to touch the doorknob. A week passes. Octavia's sleep is feverish—a symptom of her pregnancy, Reggie reassures her. In the bathtub, she studies her swollen breasts. She watches her hands knead the tumulus of her belly. Her fingernails are cut short, like a child's. Only savagely sexual women wear three-inch blades. When they stroke an erect penis, their nails graze the translucent skin. Their breasts and stomachs are as sleek as varnished bread.

And one day, her brain burning, Octavia lumbers to the closet and flings open the door. The box is gone. She pushes past stacks of books, Reggie's golf clubs, her neglected Thighmaster, and a surfboard they've been storing for Reggie's younger brother, Lowell.

Reggie's brother. Undoubtedly Lowell has the magazines. Reggie would be too frugal to destroy them, too self-conscious to give them to a friend. Octavia can picture the solemn coming-of-age ceremony: "I, Reginald Baine, hereby pass down to you, my younger sibling, the images that have fed my secret concupiscence." Lowell would be grateful; he gives guitar lessons for a living and can hardly afford to eat, much less whack off to such a costly cornucopia of smut. Meanwhile, Octavia, who is just awakening to the possibilities of pornography, may never understand its visceral allure. She could buy her own supply, of course, but the image of a pregnant doctoral candidate buying fuck rags at a liquor store makes her cringe.

Octavia phones her brother-in-law. "Lowell," she says coldly, "Have you seen Reggie recently?"

"Hey, Octopus. I saw him Saturday, as a matter of fact. He came up with a few boxes he wanted to give me. Some clothes and stuff."

And stuff. How chivalrous. Never mention pornography to a woman; she'll launch into a feminist diatribe that will singe the eardrums. Octavia gets to the point.

"Did he give you any magazines?"

"Yes," Lowell drawls.

"With lots of pictures of genitalia?"

"Are you psychic? Or did you two have a fight over Reggie's hobby?"

"I want them back!" Octavia snaps. "I'm using them for my thesis. I'm doing a feminist deconstruction of pornography, and I was using those as my research materials."

"I thought you were writing about Emily Dickinson!" Lowell protests.

"Dickinson's poetry has an erotic subtext that the lay reader wouldn't recognize," says Octavia haughtily. "There's more than a hint of submissive sexuality in 'He put the Belt around my life,' for instance."

"So do you want the three issues of *Belts on Butts*?"

"You can keep *Belts on Butts*."

"And *The Wide World of Water Sports*?"

"We'll pick and choose when I get there. Are you busy this afternoon?"

"Come on by, baby," says Lowell.

Lowell is twenty-six years old and has never had a permanent job. Four years ago he went to LA to seek work as a studio musician. Reggie loaned his brother his Volvo and a credit card to be used for emergencies. Lowell promised to return the credit card and the car within two weeks. Three months later, he straggled back to the Bay Area on a Greyhound. He had maxed out the card, sold Reggie's car, and contracted chlamydia. Besides the infection, he brought back nothing but his beloved guitar. Reggie calmly took that, sold it, and pocketed the cash.

Octavia drives to San Francisco after a Pantagruelian lunch of cold fried chicken, liverwurst, and leftover kung pao beef. Her stomach burbles as it digests her meal—how she loves eating and its placid aftermath! Her mouth is the only orifice that gets filled anymore, she thinks sadly. She used to love a hard, slow fuck, the kind that made her pelvis rock like a Ferris wheel car. She has seen men gazing at her hungrily; she is ripe enough to eat. She fantasizes about following one of these fertility worshippers to a sordid motel, about letting him roam with tongue and fingers over her extravagant curves and savor the unusually heavy flow between her thighs. Those skyward-pointing nipples, that easy wetness, not to mention her perpetual horniness—shouldn't someone besides herself enjoy them?

Lowell lives in the Haight. After climbing the hill to his apartment, Octavia is exhausted, and she collapses gratefully on his mammalian brown sofa. Lowell grabs her feet and props them on a crate. He brings her a glass of water, then disappears into the bathroom. He comes out carrying the familiar cardboard box.

"Were you pissed off when you found this?" Lowell opens

the box and dumps its contents on the carpet, then studies Octavia's facial expression as if analyzing her reaction. "I've always admired you for being so open-minded."

"I *am* open-minded," she insists. "You of all people should know that. Remember the night I explained to you about my theory of marriage? That I had refused to marry Reggie unless he agreed that we could both include other lovers in our relationship?"

Lowell's neck and cheeks flush bright. He clears his throat. "Um, I've never forgotten it. I still think about it, in fact."

The week before Octavia and Reggie got married, Octavia had invited Lowell out for an Italian meal to celebrate their new relationship as in-laws. She thought that Lowell, like all starving musicians, would probably appreciate a free dinner, but more importantly, she wanted him to know that his brother's new marriage wasn't going to be as conventional as it might seem. Reggie had known about their dinner date, of course. He was delighted that his fiancée wanted to get to know his little brother; in fact, he hoped that Octavia would inspire Lowell to find a loving relationship of his own, one that was both stable and varied, with a rainbow of erotic possibilities in the background. But when Octavia offered to give Lowell a graphic demonstration of the possibilities of polyamory, over pasta and wine in North Beach, Lowell had been overwhelmed. Aroused beyond all reason, he had begged for a rain check and fled the restaurant, leaving a stunned Octavia to finish his serving of tiramisu.

How things have changed, Octavia thinks, sighing inwardly as she watches Lowell sift through the glossy porn mags. He had been so turned on by her nubile, unmarried body. Today, with her unwieldy belly and puffy legs, he probably thinks of her as a different species from the women in those erotic images.

"Incredible! There's a fetish for everything!" Lowell remarks. "Feet. Amazons. Women with facial hair. Did you have any idea that Reggie was a secret porn fiend?"

"No," Octavia says. "He kept the box in a closet, under our wedding album. I had no idea he was attracted to women with facial hair."

"Well, you see, these magazines usually come in packs of three. And they're wrapped in plastic, so you can only see the one on top. Poor old Reg probably slithered into an adult bookstore, snatched up a couple of three-packs, and left. It's a crapshoot. You never know exactly what you're getting."

"That's comforting," Octavia sighs. "Do you think Reggie's addicted to porn?"

"This stuff is snakefruit. Once you've sunk your teeth in, it's tough to forget the taste. Reggie probably worried about how you'd react if you found his collection, but he still has the craving. You can bet on it."

Octavia studies Lowell as he sorts through the magazines, stacking them according to fetish. He is wearing a goatee now, and his hair has grown below his shoulders. Whenever she sees Lowell, with his secondhand clothes and aimless freedom, she feels sorry for Reggie. She can imagine the boys growing up together, Reggie forever forced to be vigilant and prim, Lowell allowed to sink into voluptuous failure.

"I posed for some magazines like this," Lowell said suddenly. "I don't think I'm in any of these, though."

"You *posed* for them? My god, when?"

"When I was down in LA and starving to death. It was an okay job. I had sex with a few women and got paid for it. No big deal." Lowell's face is the color of a boiled lobster. "I think that's when I got chlamydia. It could have been a lot worse."

"I cannot believe you did that. Even without the medical

risks, it's so unlike you! Screwing total strangers, while someone took pictures of it! I can't believe that, Lowell. And you're so skinny!"

"What difference does it make that I'm skinny?" Lowell asks in a hurt tone. "I'm photogenic, in a retro-hippie kind of way."

Octavia tries to imagine Lowell posing nude with a woman—maybe two or three women. She imagines a mattress covered by a cheap polyester bedspread, pocked with cigarette burns, in a room with aggressively white walls. Before the camera rolls, the actors exchange jokes and sticks of chewing gum. The setting she envisions is about as sexy as a surgical theater.

"Was it hard to get an—uh—erection?" Octavia asks.

"Not really. The cameras didn't bother me. I thought the photographer would be some kind of space ape, but he could have worked at Disneyland. It's weird, but the only time I had a problem was when I brought in one of my girlfriends. With strangers it was easy."

"But wasn't it disturbing to make love to strangers?"

"Sometimes. One girl had a bizarre smell. I tried to be polite about it, but sheesh! It was tough. I just closed my eyes and pretended I was drinking miso soup."

Octavia shakes her head. "I can't see it. Didn't you feel cheap, or guilty, or at least sad? Didn't you think about how it could affect the rest of your life? What if you get into a high-profile career, or decide you want to start a family?"

"Right. You're looking at Mr. High-Profile Family Man."

"You could change your lifestyle someday," says Octavia defensively.

"You never know."

"Believe it or not, I did think before I tore off my clothes and launched my modeling career. I could have gotten a job flipping burgers—that would have taken care of food and money in one blow. But I *wanted* to do this. I wanted to be out there, naked. I mean, this is the closest thing I've done to art. The guitar's just a hobby. When I had the chance to be in these magazines, something inside me said, *Give it up, Lowell. All or nothing.*"

He is holding a copy of *Big 'n' Busty.* The magazine quivers in his hands. All around him lie the fruits of commitment, indifference, carelessness, need. So many bodies, so many hungers between those pages.

"I didn't mean to condemn you, Lowell," Octavia says gently.

"I know it looks sleazy. But it's the only thing I've done that was authentic. Everything else has been this half-assed floating. Trailing other people, picking up the stuff they drop. I can understand why you don't understand."

"I do, a little. I have to confess, I didn't want those magazines for my research."

"I thought that sounded kind of weird, even for you," Lowell smiles. "I knew you weren't that shallow about Emily Dickinson."

"She wasn't as genteel as you might think," Octavia says. "'Ourself behind ourself, concealed—Should startle most—'. But you can keep the magazines. I don't think I could handle a hoard of snakefruit."

Octavia shifts her weight. The apartment is cool inside, and she doesn't mind the murky light. The magazines lie strewn like shiny coloring books on the floor.

"Could I see your stomach?" Lowell asks. "I've never seen a pregnant woman's belly."

The request startles her at first, but in this atmosphere of revelation, it seems natural, even necessary, that she expose something.

"Why not?" she says, lifting her T-shirt.

"Jesus, it's a pod!" Lowell exclaims, staring at the shimmery hummock.

"Can I touch it?"

Octavia nods. Lowell kneels in front of her and runs both hands over her skin, stretched nearly to transparency. Blue veins course over the milky slopes. The tissue gleams. Octavia closes her eyes.

"I should warn you about something," Lowell says, "because you're my sister-in-law and everything."

"What?"

"I'm getting a hard-on. And I don't know why."

Octavia's eyes fly open.

"This has got to be the weirdest thing I've ever seen. It looks like a chrysalis."

He leans forward and applies his tongue to the pale globe. Slowly he encircles Octavia's stomach, then stops.

"I thought it would have, like, an arctic taste," he comments. "But it's warm."

Octavia closes her eyes again. This unveiling of her belly feels like a surreal game of show-and-tell. She knows, when Lowell raises his body and rubs his erection against the southern slope of body, that she should protest, but the contact makes her weak. Lightly his lips clasp hers, soft as a question. Now he's lifting her hair, murmuring in her ear.

"Can pregnant women have sex? I've got a condom in my wallet, and I desperately need to use it."

"Of course pregnant women can have sex. A lot of us *want* sex, believe it or not."

"You're just so fucking beautiful, Octavia. I've never wanted to be inside anyone so much. I want to get deep into you, with everything I have. Is that okay? Or am I crazy?"

"You're not crazy," she says softly. "And yes. It's okay."

She hadn't realized how much she missed being wanted, or how much she wanted to hear words like *fuck* applied to her own body. She wraps her arms around Lowell and pulls him close. His lean, slender body feels taut and hard, his muscles vibrating like the strings of a finely tuned instrument.

"We could do it as an experiment," Lowell says, mistaking her silence for hesitation. "It wouldn't be fucking, it would be more like intercourse. I promise not to hurt you."

"Fucking is what I want!" Octavia cried. "I don't want to be an experiment, and I don't want to be worshipped. Just *take* me."

"Can I lick you first? I'm fulfilling several fantasies here."

"Seriously, do you have to ask?"

Lowell helps her scoot out of her pants. For what seems like hours, his tongue weaves through the crevices of her cunt, pulling her into a dream of honey and hot milk. She unhooks her bra so that he can slide his hands underneath and rub her swollen breasts, tweaking the hard nipples. Octavia laughs softly; it's amazing that her breasts don't burst with the pleasure of it. Opening her eyes, she sees Lowell's head below the hill of her belly, and she grasps the back of his neck, coaxing him to go deeper. As his tongue slides to her clitoris, he fucks her slowly with two fingers. Her clit has never been so sensitive; it feels like a small planet, with each side delivering a different sensation in response to Lowell's tongue.

"You are wet, wet, wet," he whispers.

"Don't stop. I'll kill you if you stop."

It starts with a tingling numbness, sharp as needles, and builds to a crest of joy that's almost painful. Lowell buries his face in her as she comes, and when she reaches the very top, the baby seems to hammer the wall of her womb with its tiny heels. Lowell beams at her, his cheeks glistening with her juices.

"It's your turn," Octavia sighs, closing her eyes in the after-glow.

She hears Lowell unbuttoning his jeans and kicking them off. She hears latex squeaking as he slides the condom over his erec-tion. It takes him a few minutes to adjust himself comfortably. First he tries kneeling in front of her, then propping himself up with his hands on the back of the sofa. Finally he slides a pillow under her rear end, then brackets himself between her thighs and slowly enters her. She's tight inside, in spite of her wetness—it's been so long since she's been prodded with anything other than a speculum.

"Could you spread your legs a little wider?"

She obeys. That's better. His penis slides into her with the blunt curiosity of a child's finger. Lowell is tentative and over-cautious, but it's so good to be desired. He glides in and out a few times, but it's not going to work; he's too worried about hurting her, he says, and he's getting a fierce cramp in the back of his thigh.

"Doesn't hurt," she murmurs.

"It was only an experiment. Will you keep your eyes closed for a few more seconds?"

She opens them. Lowell is standing over her, his face strained with lust and maybe guilt, holding his stiff penis in his hand. He has taken off the condom; his cock's secretive eye is watching her.

"I told you not to open your eyes!"

"I want to see you," she says.

"I've got a Polaroid camera," he grins. "It's Reggie's. I could give you a souvenir."

"I won't forget." Octavia settles into the sofa's primordial softness. Vast and lush, it welcomes her as a member of its own species. Lowell cries out as his warm come rains over her stomach. Moistening her fingers with his fluid, Octavia draws maps of desire on the globe of her belly.

Dusk is coming on. A tide of fading sunlight spreads across Lowell's bare back. Reggie will be coming home soon, opening the door, perhaps wondering where his pregnant wife could be. Octavia knows that she will tell him about Lowell and their afternoon together, but not tonight. She wants to keep the encounter to herself for a little longer, to let the glow of Lowell's desire and admiration warm her spirit before she shares it with anyone else.

"What do you think Reggie will have to say about this?" Lowell asks, as if he is reading her mind. "I know you two have an open relationship, but I wonder if this fits his image of you as the mother of his child—hanging out at my place talking about porn and having sex."

"I'll tell him, but not tonight," Octavia says. "I want to carry this memory around with me for a little while, first. I needed this today. I've been feeling like a sacred cow with Reggie lately, too holy to be touched."

"I don't know how he could look at your body and not want to come all over you," Lowell says. "I always thought you were gorgeous, but you've gone beyond beauty now. You're . . . edible. Literally."

"Speaking of edible, I should get home soon. It's almost dinnertime." Octavia's belly rumbles at the promise of more food. "In fact, I'm so famished that I'm going to get takeout, and probably devour an appetizer on the ride home. Can I bring you something?"

"You've already satisfied all my appetites," Lowell says. "Even a few that I didn't know I had."

He walks Octavia down the hill to her car, and she's grateful; she doesn't think she could bear to see his pale form withdrawing into the dim room. To her relief, he shambles toward a coffee house after helping her into her car. Somehow it comforts her to know that he won't be spending the evening alone, even though she realizes that solitude is his preferred state of being. She turns on the radio and plays kinetic jazz to distract herself from her projections of his loneliness.

As Octavia leaves the city, the traffic thickens until her car is barely moving. Usually she panics in rush-hour traffic, but today it reassures her to be part of a slow-moving river of people, many of them tired and hungry or irritable and lonely, longing to be fed or touched. A heavyset bald man rubs his eyes in the car next to her. An elderly woman massages her neck as she sits on a bench, waiting for her bus. Octavia's baby turns in its bed of microscopic tendrils, giving her a sound kick as it dreams of its own desires.

HIM

Sommer Madsen

Adam likes to dress me for my dates. He roots through my closet while I shower, he digs through my drawers while I dry my hair. It's not uncommon to come out and find a full ensemble, including accessories, laid out on our neatly made king-size bed.

"I see you chose red," I say.

My hair is still damp and I'll leave it that way. It encourages my subtle curl.

"I did. A nice dinner deserves a nice dress, don't you think?"

I nod as I run my fingers along the silk. "I do."

He snags my wrist and pulls me closer. He runs his hands down the curve of my ass, the flare of my hips, and then kisses me. The kiss is gentle at first, then rougher.

"Have a good time tonight before you come home to me," he growls in my ear.

The wetness between my thighs, already there due to anticipation, increases tenfold.

"I will." I can feel myself blushing.

I roll my thigh-high stockings on slowly, knowing he likes to watch. How I point my toes, how the muscle in my calf flexes, how they come to rest snugly at the top my thigh. And, as always, he comes closer and runs a fingertip below the elastic-and-lace band at the top. His hand dips briefly between my thighs and brushes over my mound. His finger expertly darting out to drag across my thumping clitoris.

I take a deep breath, shut my eyes, and stand, pulling on panties and then fastening my bra. He helps me with the dress and then fluffs my hair once it's been pulled over me.

Another kiss, another skate of his hands along my curves, and then he's handing me a pair of black strappy sandals and I'm fitting my feet into them.

"Call when you're headed home," he says and then kisses the back of my neck.

The fine hair at my nape tingles, my nipples go tight.

All the way over to John's I'm thinking about Adam's hands on me.

Then John greets me at the door and his hands are on me and my mind goes blank.

He traces the outline of my hard nipples with his fingertip. "Did he choose this? Your husband?"

They don't know each other's names. There's no real reason other than I like it like that. It forces them to refer to the other as "him" and the word holds a significance, so there's an inflection that turns me on.

To John "him" is my husband, my partner, the man I swore to have and to hold.

To Adam "him" is the other. The man I fuck. My side piece. The man who I meet a few times a month to let my hair down and be good and thoroughly unattached to a vow or another person.

I always come home to him, and that's all he cares about.

I nod even as John's fingers pluck along the flare of the dress. He lifts it a little, drops it, lifts it again.

"Is it weird?" he asks, walking me back briskly until my ass hits the broad back of his sofa.

"Is what weird?" I interject, even though I know the rest of the question instinctively.

"That I like to fuck you in the clothes he picks out."

"No—and yes," I say, laughing as he turns me. He's moving me fast and it's making me wetter.

He plants my hands on the back of the sofa and I brace myself as he knocks my legs wider. His hands move along my skin like he's patting me down. He cups my pussy in one big hand, gives it a squeeze, before dragging his palms along my soft panties, the tops of my thigh-highs, down the length of my legs to finger the straps of my shoes.

He presses against me and I can feel his cock—long, hard, ready—pressing the cleft of my ass. I push back, making my excitement known.

He tugs my panties to the side and drags his finger through my wetness and then paints it over my clit. He wraps his big arm around my middle, holding me still as he strokes me. Circles, figure eights, straight lines. He works that tight knot of flesh expertly. Within minutes, I'm shuddering against him, his arm holding me steady.

"Good girl, Katherine," he says and nips my earlobe with his teeth.

John lets go of me and I brace myself again.

He peels my panties down and moves them carefully over my thigh-highs before removing them. He's behind me, chest pressed to my back, and he holds them in front of me. "He picked these?"

"Yes."

A grunt.

He pushes two fingers inside my thigh-high. "And he picked these."

This time it isn't a question.

"Yes," I whisper.

My own moisture seeps out of me, flows down, and coats the tops of my thighs. I'm that wet. My brain is drunk with it—the feeling of power and surrender in equal measure.

John hikes the dress up to my waist and I clutch at it with one hand. Holding it. Keeping myself exposed from the waist down. He drags his fingers along the thigh-highs and I feel the thin nylon bristle at his touch.

"Oops, there's a snag in there now," he growls as he peels them down.

It seems like an aggressive move. A challenge almost. And it turns me on.

My shoes are the next to go. Then his zipper sounds and my nipples turn to stones, my stomach tumbles, my pussy aches to be filled.

He pushes his fingers inside me first.

"Oh, look what a bad girl you are. Look how turned on you are with me ruining something the hubby chose. You like it?"

I nod. I gasp when his fingers flex.

"And it turns you on that he picks out these outfits?"

I don't lie. There's no reason. I nod again and there's another gasp when he bites the place where my neck and shoulder connect. Goose bumps spring up along that skin and my thighs break out with them too. I have no reason why. I don't care.

His fingers drive into me hard and fast. At one point, the force lifts me up on my tiptoes.

I chew my lower lip and try to suck in a breath.

He drags his cock along my asscrack. Draws on my asscheeks with the tip—his own little amusement. Then he's pushing against my slick opening and I widen my legs instinctively.

That big arm hooks around me again and the other hand grabs my long hair like a lead. He pushes into me and I go up on my toes again. His cock fills me, dragging along my G-spot. It's the perfect angle, the perfect pace, the perfect amount of friction. He tugs my hair and nibbles my neck and I give it up as easy as you please. I come with a soft cry, my hands clutching at nothing but air. My pussy spasms, embracing his driving flesh, flickering and flexing with every thrust.

He backs off for just a moment, just long enough to let me catch my breath. Then he turns me to face him and tugs my dress over my head—it's a bit too rough. Something rips. Not a lot. Just a little. But that brittle sound of cloth tearing is clear as a bell.

He tosses the dress and the bra in the pile, bends to scoop me up, and gets me slung over his shoulder. He drops me on the sofa gently, and pushes me back, settling over me.

His dark eyes are animalistic, his mouth a near leer, his cock so hard and flushed it steals my breath.

"There. No armor chosen by him. Just me and you. Naked. You're mine at the moment."

And he settles over me, dragging his erection along my sex. His gaze is pinned to mine and he's teasing me. He's fucking with me. He knows I want more and he knows I can't stand it.

I reach for him but he grabs my hand and pins it above my head. I reach with the other hand and he snags me again. I'm trapped there. Watching him. I smile finally and whisper, "I have to go back to him soon. Don't you want to fuck me more? Don't you want me to go home fully used and fully sated?"

There. I've played my little card. It's up to him.

He cocks his head and growls at me.

I shiver beneath him.

"You play dirty, Katherine."

I smile as he drives into me, his cock filling me, stretching me. Every thrust bangs his pelvic bone against my clit. It's a wonderful drumbeat of pressure.

He holds me there, fucks me hard, grunts and carries on. I can tell by his face that he's close. He wants to come and he wants to wait. He wants to tease me, but he wants to fuck me too. He'll have to wait close to two weeks to see me again. Date nights should be used in full.

I pull my legs up, wrap them around his waist, hook my ankles, and drive up from beneath him. His fingers squeeze my wrists and trap my pulse in its cage of flesh and bone and sinew.

I crane my neck and kiss him. I bite his lower lip and make him snarl. I clench my pussy and thrust my hips and he finally grunts, "Fuck. I'm going to come. Come with me."

I relax just a little and feel the tip of his cock brushing the tender places I need it most and when he stiffens over me, his mouth parted, his eyes softening, his gaze full of adoration, I come. The sensation of it trips him up and he lets go, muttering, "Fuck—"

We lie there in a heap for a moment before he looks up at me and kisses my mouth. "The earrings?"

I smile. "Yes."

"Damn it. I missed those."

He brushes my lips with his thumb then covers my nipple with his mouth.

"Do you think it's strange?"

"What?" I ask.

But I know.

"That him picking the clothes gets me off—us off—and fuels our fucking?"

I shrug. "No stranger than the fact that him choosing my outfit gets him off. And later will fuel *our* fucking."

John nods. "Get up. Let's eat. And then we'll revisit this. I want to peel that slightly tattered dress off you and eat that pussy."

I take his hand and help him gather my clothes so we can get there in time to make our reservation. "I think that sounds like the perfect ending to date night."

SPEED PLAY

Abigail Ekue

"Here's your ballot." The cheerful plus-size woman at the registration desk hands the man a notepad as she continues with her explanation. "You'll mark off which dates you are interested in seeing again after today. Each woman has a number. Any questions?"

"Just one, what's *your* number?"

The host giggles. The charm bomb strikes again. "You silly!" He may be silly but he's down for bouncing off her cushion all night long.

Mark enters the main dining room of the restaurant, which has been reconfigured for the speed-dating event. And with Mark's looks he'll likely be snapped up at the speed of sound. In the world of singles in his city, men are outnumbered by women. The world is his for the taking, at least tonight, since he's at an event to actually meet someone with similar intentions.

Mark is six-foot-three and a solid two hundred and ten pounds. He works in IT consulting but flaunts his mailroom-clerk looks. The blue-collar sex appeal works to his advantage. He learned in college that looking like a dummy with smarts was his key to success. Professors and the women who gave him pussy were always sucked into the illusion—this isn't a man I have to fix, he's already "there." He has no children or emotional baggage that they can discern before their intense passionate flings die out.

The room buzzes with conversation once the event is underway. Couples sit face-to-face at the dating stations, getting to know as much as they can about one another in five minutes before deciding if they want to see each other again. Countless situationships and legit marriages can trace their origin stories back to this speed-dating event. There's an attractive mix of Black and Latino singles paired up. It makes you wonder why any of these people are single, if only for the sole reason that they'd look scrumptious in their leaked sex tapes.

The signature voice of D'Angelo singing the line, "How does it feel?" echoes throughout the space. The event host bounces to the center of the room. "Okay, fellas! Time's up! If you'd like to see your dates again, don't forget to mark down her badge number or"—she makes air quotes—"*digits,* so we can arrange your real-life dates." She chuckles, proud of her form of branding for this event. "Now, move to the"—more air quotes—"*dating booth* to your right and begin your next date!"

Mark's next date is with Jehina. She's caramel, almost a golden hue with blonde dreadlocks. Her burgundy-stained lips excite him. He leans forward with his elbows on the table. Jehina's textbook posture accentuates her breasts, making them appear a full cup larger. She maintains expectant eye contact with him. He checks off her number on his ballot before the first word is even uttered.

At the neighboring dating booth, Roz, thirty-one, is engaged in intense conversation with an average-sized, light-skinned man named Chase, whose prominent feature is his bulbous eyes. His gaze can penetrate anyone when angered but melt your heart when he's in the mood to play. He's a departure from her previous speed date with a man who looked like he had a history of doing gay porn.

"I sing. It's my life force," he explains in response to her *What do you do?* query.

"That's an interesting way to put it, your life force."

"Think about it, the breathing, the energy transfer, the emotions, the healing power. It's all there when you sing. And the healing power of music has been proven."

Roz has had her fill of men who tread the surface and don't dive deep into life. She was getting the impression that Chase could handle emotions without feeling like it would challenge his manhood. At twenty-eight, Roz already had her own business, had sold two previous entrepreneurial ventures for a substantial amount, and had traveled the world via airports and her pussy.

She leans back in her seat to take in more of the scene before her. "I could see you singing your children to sleep one day. Or singing your daughter down the aisle."

Chase hadn't even thought that far ahead in his own life. But he's at speed dating to connect with any women to possibly get there. "Roz, I'm gonna go ahead and check your badge number right now." He makes the notation on his ballot with a playful flourish.

Roz reaches into her handbag, this time for her business card instead of a stick of gum. She slides it stealthily across the table. "Chase, I'm gonna go ahead and give you my number right now."

Chase's eyes dart around the room while he picks up her card and slips it into his pocket.

This round, The Weeknd summons the singles to make their way to their next dates. Mark studies the woman sitting two booths away, overlooking the date right in front of him. He tries to catch Chase's eye in the hopes they can switch places but he's already sitting with his next date. Mark sits down across from Roz. They eye each other while the host of the event gives a pep talk. Once the timer starts on their date, they continue to stare at each other.

"Hey."

"Hey."

"This is a cool event." She places her hands on the table, interlocking her fingers.

Mark nods. "Yeah, it's good to see all these beautiful people together."

Roz twirls her thumbs as if hitting a mini–speed bag. Not that the man sitting across from her isn't one of the beautiful people, but it appears both of them have run out of steam for the evening.

"Listen, I kinda already met someone tonight I'm interested in. I mean, sure, I could meet more than one person, it's just . . ."

"Oh! Great! Me too . . . I already know who I want." Mark quickly amends his statement so it doesn't sound as one-track as he may have meant it. "I already know who I'd like to see again for a real date, you know?"

"So we don't have to pretend . . ." Their expressions dissolve into relaxed smiles.

Roz and Chase return to her downtown high-rise apartment. Her three-tiered twenty-five-watt floor lamp lights the room. In the dim glow, Chase scans the room like a lemur on the lookout for fossa, checking out the luxury furnishings and overall upscale quality of the apartment. The double glass doors leading to the terrace are closed but the curtains are open, allowing city lights to cast shadows throughout the room.

"So what do you like on your tongue, Chase?"

His back stiffens and his arms drop straight to his sides. "I was taking a look at some of your art—wait, what?" He cocks his head to one side. "Did you just ask what I would like on my tongue?"

Roz places a bottle of Johnnie Walker Blue on the bar along with two glasses. "Alexa, turn on the music." An even sultrier version of Chris Isaak's "Wicked Game" massages the air between Chase and Roz. She sways and fixes the drinks.

He approaches the bar. "I need a splash of water in mine." He fends off her protests by putting up his hand. "I know . . . but I need to protect my instrument," he touches his throat.

Roz resigns herself with a nod and adds a splash of water to his drink. She joins him on the other side of the bar. "Cheers! Or *salamati* as they say in Iran." They clink glasses with lusty eye contact.

"You've been to Iran too?"

"Yeah, I spent time traveling through Iran, Turkey, Cyprus, and Greece."

"That is outstanding." He sips his whisky.

She places her drink down. "I've never had Johnnie with water. How does it taste?" She fans her fingers on the back of his head and neck and pulls him in for a kiss. When his body crashes into hers, his drink sloshes around in his glass, a few drops landing on his hand and wrist. He blindly places the glass on the bar then picks her up and sits her on the bar. She loves the feeling of her hips and thighs spreading out over the cool marble. She wraps her legs around his thighs and they explore each other's mouths, necks, and bodies. She pulls her shirt off over her head without disturbing a single hair in her auburn-highlighted TWA. His hands and tongue are on her bare breasts before she can bring her arms down.

As quickly as his mouth finds her breast, her hands wrestle with his belt buckle and pants button.

"I'll give it to you . . ." he says half in her mouth as he unzips his pants. His hands send his pants down and her hands scoop his dick out from his underwear.

She breaks the kiss to look at him. The two have their foreheads pressed together as they gaze down at his body.

"It's pretty . . ." He's a little over seven inches and fat. She strokes it, crooning, "Wow . . ." Her fingers swirl under his balls.

"Yeah?"

"Fuck yeah . . ." She's stroking him again.

"Are you pretty?" He cups her crotch with his hand and sticks his tongue in her mouth again.

Mark and Jehina enter from the foyer. "Oh! I'm so sorry!" Jehina shrieks and hides her face against Mark's shoulder. There's a mass scramble to avoid eye contact and cover up exposed body parts.

Roz drapes her arm over her breasts. She shoos Chase from in front of her so she can jump down while he's buttoning his pants. She turns her back to the others and puts her top back on. Mark and Chase don't speak while they eyeball each other.

"Um, can I go—where's your washroom?"

"Third door. End of the hall," Mark says. His date makes a hasty retreat from the living room. Mark stares at the man who's concentrating on him so hard that he doesn't even sneak a look at his date from behind as she walks away. Instead, Roz does the scoping of Jehina's hourglass figure accentuated by the electric-blue pencil skirt she's wearing. She has a body that would make a man forget his baby in the backseat.

Roz unnecessarily adjusts her clothes. She has the focus of

someone rehearsing lines from a play. "Chase, this is Mark. He lives here too."

"Hey, how's it going, man?" Chase extends his hand. The men shake hands.

"He's my husband." Roz watches the impact of the bomb she just dropped. Chase drops his chin, squeezing his eyes shut and tries to shake his head clear. When he opens his eyes again he looks directly at Mark.

"Hey, dude, I'm so sorry. She didn't tell me she was—"

"No, it's okay, I knew she was here with you." Mark smiles.

Roz and Mark say *we got him* with their shared glance. She places her hand on Chase's back. "I brought you over here thinking we all could . . ."

"Whoa! Whoa, whoa, whoa, whoa . . ." He backs away from the couple. "I'm gonna go get some air." He rushes out to the terrace.

Roz doesn't have to say a word to express that that didn't go as planned. "What did *your* date say?" she asks.

"I didn't tell her yet."

The battle to give Mark a piece of her mind or to hold her peace is written all over her face. She exhales audibly.

"That's the dude you want tonight?"

"Yeah." Her tone says she doesn't appreciate her choice being questioned. Mark's never had an issue with her dates before. As he reaches for his wife to make peace, they hear the bathroom door open.

"I'm gonna go talk to him." She makes her retreat to the terrace.

Jehina peeks into the living room from the hall. Mark smiles and waves her in. "The coast is clear."

"Sucks we walked in on your roommate like that. Hope we're not in the way of him and his date."

"Actually, *he's* not my roommate. I live with her."

Slight discomfort flashes across her face. But her acceptance of the living situation is written in her expression soon after.

"She's my wife."

"Naw. How the fuck you gonna bring me home after meeting me at a speed-dating event for single people? And hold up! She was in here messing around with some dude! Yo . . . ya'll are some freaks!"

"I brought you home with me because I want you. I'm not a freak."

"But ya'll are married. Like what the fuck yo?"

"Right. Happily married for eight years. I love Roz with all my heart. She's all I need in a woman"—Jehina rolls her eyes at this—"but that doesn't mean I don't want other women. I'm human. And I'm a fucking *man*."

"Yeah, and just like a fucking man, you gotta fuck around." She crosses her arms over her chest.

"Aight be easy. I'm not fucking around on my wife. I would never do that."

Her upper lip curls like she's been hit with a whiff of something rotten and her eyes hop around the room looking for the source of the rank odor. "Well I guess if you're gonna cheat, you might as well have it out in the open."

"It's not cheating *because* it's out in the open. We don't have secrets."

Jehina looks toward the terrace at Roz and Chase. "So you're telling me you're fine with your woman fucking other dudes?"

"She's not *mine*. I don't own her. But yes, I'm fine with it. She's very in tune with who she is sexually. And ya'll women be wanting *a lot* more than one man can give."

Jehina can't help but crack a smile at that tidbit from Mark because it rings true for her. "So ya'll just get horny and swing?"

"We're in an open marriage. But yes, sometimes we swing. She's had boyfriends, I've had girlfriends . . ." He shrugs off this fact of life while conveniently leaving out that his girlfriends are usually only around for one night.

She uncrosses her arms and drops her bag onto the couch. "And ya'll thought it was a good idea to go snag some fresh meat from the butcher shop." She shakes her head.

"Aight, full disclosure," he says, and sits on one of the bar stools. "Yes, we went out tonight because we wanted to play. So we registered for the speed dating. That way we could meet people who had something going on in their lives and in their heads and who we also wanna fuck."

"You checked off my number before you even spoke to me. Don't think I didn't see that."

"I *said* part of the criteria was it had to be someone we wanted to fuck. And you fine as all get-out, girl."

They laugh. Mark waves her over to the bar and takes her hand when she's within reach. "We can go slow. Whatever you wanna do. But I was hoping we all could play tonight."

Her eyes dart back toward the terrace. "He's not bad looking . . ."

"See . . . ?"

"But I'm not interested in another woman's coolie. No disrespect to your wife, *at all*, it's just not my thing."

"You've never explored with a woman?"

"I guess that's one of the things you forgot to ask me on our date," she mocks with wide eyes and a neck roll. She picks up one of the glasses of Johnnie left on the bar by Chase and Roz.

"Wait . . . I didn't pour those."

"You're talking about me eating a woman's pussy. Does it really matter?" She raises the glass to her lips.

Chase lights a cigarette. His shoulders are up at his ears and he's hugging himself despite the seventy-degree temperature outside. He glances at Roz when she joins him on the terrace.

"Why do you smoke? You're a singer."

He takes a long drag from his cigarette and lets the smoke escape his full, pursed lips. "I only do this when I'm nervous."

"You must be nervous a lot." Roz is enthralled at his expert handling of the cigarette.

It takes Chase a few seconds to catch her meaning. "And that's why I sing." He flashes a half smile.

"Ah, vicious cycle." She glances back into the apartment at the faint sound of her husband and his date laughing at the bar. When she turns her attention back to Chase, he's also watching the scene in the apartment.

"Hey, I need to apologize to you. I should've told you what was going on before we got to this point."

"You're a woman who knows what she wants. And you got it. I'm here." He takes another drag of the cigarette.

Roz struggles to read the expression on his profile. "So, um, my husband and I were looking to play tonight."

"I liked playing with you."

She looks back into the apartment and sees Mark has his arm around Jehina. He's whispering something in her ear and judging by the smile on her face, Roz knows her husband's date is gushing in her panties. He has a way with words and his hands that women can't resist. Jehina exudes a demure aura that coming from the right woman is like catnip for Mark. Nibbling on her neck is just icing on the cake. One down, one to go. Roz turns her attention back to Chase. He quickly turns his attention back toward the night skyline of the city.

"I gotta be upfront though." She props her elbows on the railing. "I don't think you're gonna be able to play one-on-one with Mark."

"Why would I want—"

Roz cuts him off with a shake of her head sparing him from hemming and hawing his way through a bogus explanation. Chase turns his whole body to face her. "How'd you know?" He puffs on his cigarette.

"I could just sense it." She shrugs.

"Even though I was hooking up with you?"

"Doesn't mean you don't want to hook up with him too. It's cool. Some of us are bi. No crime in that." She watches as he takes a deep breath, his shoulders shrugging even higher. "Plus it's not like you ran outta here when we told you. I think you were hoping it was more than just a swap." Since the couple decided to explore other people together, her husband has never played with her male dates. He had no issue being naked with another man, being ringside while they smashed her, but that was as far as he ever went.

"So he's never . . . ever?"

Roz sends her eyes skyward in a moment of total recall. "Well, this one time, at band camp . . ." Chase laughs at the movie reference before she breaks and laughs too. "But seriously, when we first got into the lifestyle we went to a festival. Turned out to be this pan/poly event. At night, they had bonfires, spankings, and skinny-dipping but there was also a boom boom room."

Every visible part of Chase's body perks up at the mention of the boom boom room. She nods in agreement with his excitement as she remembers. "Yeah, so there was this dude who really liked me, but," she turns her head toward the city and lowers her voice a bit, "he also wanted to get fucked by Mark."

The gleam in Chase's eye is undeniable as he drops his arms for the first time. Roz stomps on his dreams the way he extinguishes a smoldering cigarette butt. "He teased and denied both of us that night." She shakes her head. "I would've loved to have seen that." She turns and leans against the railing, facing the apartment. "He's a great fuck."

Chase takes the last drag of his cigarette, the embers racing toward his fingers as he cradles his body even tighter. She's thrilled by the roll of his hip when he crushes the cigarette under the toe box of his shoe. "I knew I liked you."

"Yeah?"

"Yeah, you have an intuitive, nurturing energy that I was attracted to tonight. I could tell you live by that 'one love' philosophy."

"We both read each other tonight."

He practically melts into a puddle when she places her hand on his back. He wraps his arm around her shoulders. "Wanna know how Dunhills taste?" he lifts her chin and they pick up where they left off on the bar.

Mark and Jehina are rounding the bases on the couch. He's already stripped down to his underwear and has helped her out of her blouse and bra. Her back arches when he eases her nipple into his mouth. She squeezes him tighter with her thighs in response to his suckling. He moves attentively down her body. His fingers travel under her skirt and under the front of her cotton panties. His pelvis presses forward when his finger parts her pussy lips. He's eager to put his dick where his finger is exploring. He kisses her softly and she sucks on his tongue.

"Yeah, go slow . . . like that . . ." She grips his wrists as she trembles. He slowly pulls his finger out and wastes no time putting it in his mouth.

His eyes light up. "Damn, you delicious . . ." He sucks his finger clean. Jehina is wearing her skirt like a belt by the time he grabs her by the hips and whips her body around so he can bury his face between her legs.

Roz leads Chase back into the apartment and they're mesmer-ized by the scene playing out before them.

Mark comes up for air. "You ever tasted yourself?" His shiny face is a sight long overdue. Her bed has been cold for a long time.

Roz kisses his shoulder and she feels him up with the reach-around. "Her pussy looks so hot, babe." Jehina's golden pussy with her trimmed, natural dark-brown hair is almost too much stimuli for Roz.

Jehina draws her knees together slightly at the sight of Roz kissing and sucking on Mark's neck. Having a man's wife at the party while she receives some of the best head she's ever had is new territory for her. It doesn't help that Roz is about to dive headfirst into her pussy too.

Mark stands, says, "Taste . . ." and kisses Jehina. She kisses her juices from his lips, chin, and cheeks. She flinches at the sensation of Roz's hand on her thigh but Mark reads her sudden movement as hunger for more. He drops to his knees and licks her again, stiffening his muscular tongue and dipping it into her.

"Gimme some . . ." His wife's lips are parted waiting for him to give her a taste of his date. While the married couple shares Jehina's flavor, she guides Roz's hand off her leg.

"You *are* sweet, hon . . ." Roz smiles at her. She stands and brings Mark to his feet too. She notices Jehina's hips and belly relax at the sight of her husband. She takes hold of him in his boxer briefs, her fingers and thumb nowhere near touching as she wraps them around him. Jehina's eyes dart back and forth like she's tracking a fast-moving target. Roz rakes her fingers down the front of her husband's body, biting her bottom lip, and grants Jehina permission with a nod. The two women bond while they run their hands on Mark's chest.

Roz purrs approvingly at the sight of Jehina working her clit in a circular motion. Jehina smiles slyly at being caught.

Mark is wet in Roz's hands from the stroking. "You ready to show her, baby?" She continues to stroke him. "You ready to show her what you got?" She pushes the waistband of his boxer briefs below his ball sac. He salutes both women with his rigid nine inches, the head shiny from his precum.

"Shit . . ." Jehina thinks for a second that she's bitten off more than she can handle, but she's too fired up to stop now.

Roz follows her gaze to Chase who's rubbing himself over his pants. She reaches out to him, inviting him to come closer. "Get over here . . ." She playfully runs her tongue along her teeth while stroking Mark, sharing her true meaning with Chase. And he loves her for it. He wraps his arms around her. She tips her face back toward him and they kiss sloppily.

"This is Chase," she says, and looks down at the other woman. "You might remember him from earlier . . ." she teases. Up close, Jehina realizes she really likes his face, his large eyes giving him a piercing gaze. There's sexual prowess in his eyes. His lips are swollen from kissing Roz.

"Taste my husband, beautiful." She points Mark's dick down toward Jehina, who takes as much of him as she can into her mouth.

"Nnnnh . . ." Mark feels like he's being wrapped in a hot towel. His sounds trigger Chase, who gropes Roz's tits from behind while she grinds her ass against him. "I want summa that . . ." The wet whisper in her ear is proof of his hunger for her husband.

She turns to face Chase and frees him from his pants for the second time that evening. "This is gonna be fun." Her comments directed at his dick. He steals glances at Mark, who's lost in the sensations of Jehina's tongue up, under, and around his dick and balls. Her burgundy lip stain is all but gone and is replaced by the blood engorging her lips. Mark hangs on to her by two handfuls of her golden locks and rocks his hips into her face. She does a good job holding him deep in her throat until she has to back off for air.

The sound of the wet release draws Roz's attention. "Damn, she got you, baby."

"You think you can do better?" Mark challenges.

"You mind?" She checks with Chase about stopping their slow grind.

"Nah, I got her." Chase lightly rubs Jehina's chin and is lucky enough to graze Mark's balls in the process. Even as Jehina takes her first taste of him, he looks right at Mark. His gaze drops to witness Roz swallowing most of her husband's dick on the first try. He makes a mental note of how Mark likes to be sucked. Chase has the same tight grip on Jehina's dreadlocks that Mark had earlier and his ass clenches while she controls him with dick-length sucks. Raunchy and nonsensical words escape his lips while she goes berserk on his dick.

For a few seconds, Roz absentmindedly strokes her husband as she watches Jehina devouring Chase. She can't help but reach for Jehina's upper inner thigh. Mark strokes his wife's head to get her attention and narrows his eyes at her. She gets the message and takes her hand off Jehina's thigh, albeit after another caress and squeeze. He just had to choose a date who wasn't into girls—that made her want her more.

Roz goes to a barn door curio cabinet and returns to the party with a handful of colorful packets. She showers the couch with the condoms as if they've been beaten out of a piñata. She has a one-track mind that's focused on getting pounded by both of the dicks in the room that night and hopefully getting a taste of pussy direct from the source.

Before too long, Chase rolls a condom on and is pushing Roz's shoulders down to the couch. "You want this deep, girl?" He slides in with an *oooh* at how snug and wet she is.

Mark sits on the couch and Jehina still has him in her mouth. He enjoys his momentary role of cuckold as Chase drills his wife. Roz joins the party when she can, slurping up and down the side of her husband's thick dick. She's aware of how deftly Jehina avoids touching her lips to hers while they both fellate her husband. Ordinarily, she'd steal her kiss anyway but she's getting off on her hard-to-get routine. The reward will be so much sweeter when she willingly gives it to her.

She revels in watching Jehina ride her husband's dick. The slap of her hips onto his thighs acts as a metronome for the room. Her sweat mixes with his. He slaps her ass hard and feels a surge of her warmth surround him. He slaps her ass again. "You like that shit, don't you?" he murmurs, and slaps her again as she continues to bounce up and down on his lap. "Let her do it . . ." he hisses at her and slaps her ass again. She's too far gone in her trance to object. "Go for it, babe . . ." he says, egging on his wife. Roz rubs her ass before slapping it with an open hand. She feels the reverb of Jehina's jelly all the way up her arm.

Before she can think, Chase pulls out of her and pushes her face into the couch next to Jehina's knee. His strong tongue on her asshole takes her breath away. His spit and her unstoppable flow leak down her thighs.

Jehina is the loudest person in the room as she coats the base of Mark's dick and balls with more of her pussy cream with each bounce. Chase locks eyes with Mark over his wife's hump. His gaze remains steady on him as he fucks Roz's ass with his tongue. It's unnerving to Mark, those doe-eyes begging for more, begging for more from *him*.

Jehina slows her bounce. "You good?" She rocks her hips trying to wake up Mark's softening dick.

Her hushed urgency snaps him out of the stare down with Chase. "Yeah"—he slaps her ass again—"get it . . . go for yours . . ." She revs up her hips again.

Basking in her afterglow, Jehina throws her head back over the arm of the couch and opens her mouth for Mark to drop his balls in. She lightly taps her pussy with her four fingers through her subtle aftershocks. Roz touches her thigh and can feel her orgasm has cleared all the resistance from her body.

On the next pass of her hand, she ends up with Jehina's juices on the tip of her finger. Jehina moans on Mark's dick. He smiles at his wife knowing the more she touches her, the better his blow job and tea-bagging will get. She traps Jehina's fat pussy lips and clit in the V of her fingers and slides up and down before slipping the tip of her finger into her wet muscle.

Jehina lifts her head briefly to see Roz is the one reigniting her. Roz sticks her finger back inside, daring her to say something. Jehina's mouth hangs open while Roz fingers her slowly, pulling out every few thrusts to ice-skate over her lips and clit with her tender fingertips. Jehina drops her head back and sucks Mark into her mouth. Roz withdraws her wet finger and runs it along Chase's lips like she's applying lipstick. She kisses him and sends him over to Mark with a jut of her chin.

The two men stand dick to dick over their Goldilocks. Roz licks the length of Jehina's pussy then blows on it. An arousing sense of pride washes over her as she tastes her husband's date. From the sounds of things, Jehina is enjoying the taste of Roz's date too. She takes a break and Jehina lets out a whimper in protest. "I'll be right back." She gives her thigh a reassuring squeeze before getting off the sofa.

She returns carrying a lifelike dildo. The way she caresses it would make any man envious. The real men in the room have their dicks pressed together by Jehina who licks the underside of both their hoods. Mark is in his own world and misses the look shared between his wife and Chase. Chase stands dick-to-dick with Mark and his smile says that counts for something. If how she's felt all evening trying to get a taste of Jehina is a fraction of the pent-up energy Chase was experiencing she knew something would have to give.

She kneels on the couch between Jehina's gaping thighs licking her pussy a little more then rubs the head of the dildo along her wide slit. Jehina answers by rocking her hips up and down. She presses the head of the dildo at her pussy opening and waits. Her hips rock some more, impatient.

"You want this, hon?" Roz is going to make her say it.

Jehina nods and mumbles her answer while switching back and forth between the two rock-hard dicks.

"Yeah? You want it?" She rubs the other woman's clit as she pushes the dildo inside her. The job Jehina is doing on the men becomes disjointed as her concentration is tested. "Mmmm . . . you're pushing me out . . ." Roz is steady as she fills Jehina with the dildo repeatedly. She squeezes one of Jehina's tits then slaps it lightly. "Let me in . . ." she coaxes. She rises up off her heels for more leverage.

Jehina has completely abandoned the men as she crescendos, a tight grip on her breast. They keep their dicks hard, masturbating at the women's heads.

"Huh? Like that? Want me to fuck you like that?" she says as she swirls the dildo on each in and out motion. Roz leans over her, bringing her lips tantalizingly close to hers. "Look at me . . ." Jehina struggles to lift her heavy eyelids. "Look at me when you come." The scent of whisky and her husband commingle on Jehina's breath as she quietly exhales her orgasm.

Roz is on the brink herself, the evidence leaking down her thigh. She stretches her body over Jehina's to lick the two throbbing heads. She spends a little more time on Mark's dick out of habit.

"So fucking . . . yes . . . Jesus . . ." Mark barely finds the words for his wife.

"Can you tell when I'm sucking you or when she's sucking you?" She sucks Chase waiting for his answer.

"Fuck, it *all* feels good . . ."

Without question she kisses Jehina, lingering for a second to let her think about it, no tongue but open-mouth. She slowly pulls the dildo out of her. "That was beautiful, wasn't it baby?" That question is for both her husband, his shoulder bouncing as he strokes himself, and the woman under her. "Damn," she says, examining the cream-coated dildo, "look at that come . . ."

Chase grabs her wrist and puts the dildo in his mouth. The married couple exchange a stunned glance as he takes the dildo from her and works it at all angles.

"I bet that'd feel good to you too, babe . . ." Roz nuzzles her face next to Chase, eyeing her husband, getting a small taste of the dildo. "You probably wouldn't even be able to tell the difference."

Chase bobs his head a few more times only leaving behind his saliva on the toy.

"You like the taste of pussy," Mark baits Chase in a pussy-loving bro moment.

"I like the taste of pussy on *dick*." Chase twirls his wrist, waving the dildo by his face.

Mark's stroking slows to a crawl then halts as his gaze floats from mouth to mouth to mouth. His wife had a knack for picking people who knew how to party.

BETWEEN
TWO LOVERS

Thomas S. Roche

She shouldn't have worn something slutty.

It had made sense early that morning. *Get them both out to brunch*, she figured, *and wear something slutty. Get them tipsy at* Verts Déchirées *(best mimosas in town, and where else can you get a breakfast salad?)—and wear something slutty. They're men. They'll go for it, duh. Don't apologize; be honest about how you feel, about the two of them, about the two coincident relationships; about sex. If you mention it to one of them before the other, it'll forever nag at the other one. Just tell them both at once, and wear something slutty.*

Without the wearing something slutty part, it ran the risk of becoming all process, no sex. And Avery hated to process. She did, however, like sex.

So she wore something slutty.

"Well," Luke chortled, "*I'm* straight!" He sounded self-congratulatory.

Avery fixed him with a gaze that could have frozen Vesuvius.

"Well, I had planned on being there," she said. "So I don't see how that matters."

"Hey, I'm not homophobic!" bleated Luke, having an urban-sensitive, new-age-guy, straight male homophobia panic.

Jacob grinned lasciviously.

"I'm not either," said Jacob. He clapped Luke on the back. "Promise you'll stay between us, Ave? Maybe we can use, like, sheets with holes in them—like the Mormons."

"Jews," said Avery.

"Excuse me?"

"Jews. Orthodox Jews are supposed to have sex through a sheet. They don't."

"I thought it was the Amish," said Luke.

"They don't either," said Avery.

"So it's not Mormons?" said Luke.

"I was making a joke," said Jacob sourly.

"Hey, guy, there's nothing wrong with gay sex," spat Luke suddenly, with a self-righteously liberal air.

"Oh, I *love* gay sex," said Jacob. "I eat it up! Nothing I love like a big fat dick!"

Luke stared at Jacob, confused.

"Not really," said Jacob sheepishly. Avery was more than a little satisfied to see him turn a deep pink.

"Look," said Avery. "Forget I said anything."

Jacob recovered: "Hey, let's not be too hasty here. I mean, we've got sexual chemistry, the two of us." He added hastily, "*Avery and me!*" in a bark, violently waving his hand to indicate—without question—that he and Luke did *not* have sexual chemistry. Then, to Avery, pointedly: "I mean, It's intense, am I right? Maybe it'll spill over and . . . you know . . ." he made a cryptic gesture describing a triangle between the three of them, talking with his hand where his tongue seemed to fail him.

"You know, *what*?" asked Avery, annoyed.

"You know."

"I *don't* know."

"This thing could work," he finally said, his voice a deep dark chocolate purr of suggestive energy. "A threesome, like you said."

"That would be weird," said Luke.

"Forget I said anything," said Avery, and gulped the second half of her mimosa.

Jacob peered at her, refilling her flute from the pitcher.

"It could work," said Jacob, to Luke. "I mean—look how she's dressed."

"Ain't *that* a fact," said Luke.

Jacob's leer radiated open lust, as his eyes took in Avery's face and upper body, the tight soft shawl-collar top molded to the outline of her breasts, her chickens stiffening her undercarriage effectively, but not as effectively as Jacob's lustful gaze stiffened her nipples. In an instant, she knew they were visible, not just because she could feel the tight hot hardness, but because Jacob and Luke exchanged a glance that told her so. She felt a wave of hot-cold-hot; her face was red, she knew. She was blushing. She shouldn't have worn something slutty. That was stupid. And as for proposing a threesome? That was fucking *stupider* than stupid.

She looked down. Her hot skin goose-bumped. She squirmed uncomfortably under the two men's gazes. Her jeans were too tight and rubbed her places she really oughtn't to be rubbed right now. She wasn't quite down to her skinny jeans, and in any event, there was less to these jeans to begin with than there ever should have been at brunch.

She felt reckless, sick, nauseated.

When she looked up, Jacob and Luke were both staring at her: shameless, ravenous, consumed by lust—word up. From the way they were drooling, if there hadn't been a table full of mimosas and fucking breakfast salads between their crotches and their faces, Avery thought both dudes would be on their way to the hospital with boner-induced chin fractures.

"Is she hot, or what?" said Luke.

"Fuckin' *smoking*," said Jake.

Christ, boys, want a drool cup? she thought bitterly, trying to fight off the wave of immense gratification. As awkward as it was, she found it fucking hot to have two guys she was totally into—and, in fact, already sleeping with—looking at her with such open lust. For a moment she wasn't sure she really wanted to stop it.

"I don't think it's that weird," said Jacob. "She's fucking hot."

"She's fucking hot," repeated Luke, nodding fervently.

"I mean, who wouldn't want to fuck her?"

"Fucking *hot*," Luke repeated.

"Forget I said anything," murmured Avery.

"I mean, is sex with her the fucking bomb or what?"

"The fucking bomb," said Luke.

"Forget I said anything," whimpered Avery.

"The things she does?"

"The things she says," purred Luke.

They high-fived. "The things she *says!*" cried Jacob merrily.

"The mouth on that girl!"

"At the right moment," said Jacob.

"She'll say the right thing—"

The dudes fist-bumped.

"But, you know, that's not what I like about her. Mostly it's the body," said Jacob.

"It's a good body," said Luke.

"Not like that. The way she moves. The way she reacts."

"Oh, yeah, yeah, yeah, yeah, yeah, yeah, fuck yeah," said Luke, consumed. "The way she *reacts*."

"I mean, erogenous?"

"Erogenous zone," grinned Luke. "One big one."

"Called Avery."

"Now you guys are just fucking with me," growled Avery.

"You know that part in the small of her back," said Jacob—whapping the back of his hand against Luke's shoulder in open camaraderie—"where if you tickle it real lightly or kinda lick it there, she just goes fucking nuts?"

"I don't know that spot," said Luke, bewildered.

"I'll show it to you," said Jacob lasciviously. "Avery, c'mere."

"Fuck off," she breathed.

Both Luke and Jacob grinned.

Luke said, "You find that place at the ball of her foot?"

"What place?"

"Like you were saying with her back. Just tickle it, or run your tongue over it, and this girl goes—"

"Forget I said anything," Avery hissed.

"—fucking nuts," mewled Luke. "The tongue especially."

"Dude, are you a fucking foot freak?"

"Hey, lighten up," said Luke. "You were just saying you wanted to suck my dick."

"Ha! I don't know what you think you heard, dude—but you heard something I didn't say. Wishful thinking?"

"Yeah, on your part."

The two made mocking kissy faces at each other.

"Forget I said anything," said Avery. "This was stupid."

Both men ignored her; their twin gaze only got progressively more obscene as the silence weighed them down.

"Personally, I'm into her tits," Luke finally said.

"Luke, *stop*." She was shifting uncomfortably.

Jacob made that sound that "dudes" make: sort of a *chaw!* sound, meaning "Yeah, no fucking shit, of course, fuck yeah, dude," or something like that. "What's not to like," he elaborated. "Perfect. Are they fucking perfect or what?"

"Forget I said anything," said Avery.

Luke: "Fucking perfect."

"Sensitive," said Jacob.

"Sure, not just visually perfect," agreed Luke.

"But, like, *sensually* perfect."

"Forget I said anything," Avery murmured.

"The way she reacts?"

"Oh, yeah. You know she can cum from her nipples—"

"Jacob! Luke! *Stop!*" she hissed. She could barely move, she was so nervous; the faint swirl of a mild mimosa-drunk did little to help. She couldn't believe she'd actually suggested this; she couldn't believe she thought that it would work. And most of all, for the thousandth time, she wished she hadn't worn something so slutty.

Avery was aware of a sudden throb in her clit; she felt clammy, *down there*; the seam of her jeans pressed in tight, reminding her that she was wearing even less by way of underwear under her too-tight, too-low-slung jeans than she wore beneath her too-tight, too-thin shawl-neck sweater. And that only made things worse.

When Avery glanced up again, the two men were staring at her tits, openly lustful. When they took in the sight of her face, red and humiliated, they both obviously felt a great deal of pleasure at seeing her humbled.

"You guys are just fucking with me."

"Speaking only for myself," said Luke. "I think we're mostly serious."

"I'm pretty serious," agreed Jacob.

"Fuck off. Offer rescinded."

"You opened the door, Ave," said Jacob.

"Yeah? Forget I did."

Then Luke said it, in his richest let's-go-to-bed voice: "You want us to *beg*?"

Jacob: "I think she wants us to beg."

"I *don't*," she said. "It was a dumb idea. I don't know what I was thinking."

"You were the one who wanted to date us both," said Luke.

"Yeah, after you broke up with me!"

"She's got a point there, dude," said Jacob.

Luke: "Yeah, well . . . that was stupid."

"And now you gotta pay the price for your indiscretion," said Jacob, in his "Dr. Evil" voice.

The two high-fived.

"That place on her back," asked Luke. "You'll show it to me?"

"Oh, *fully*, dude, I'll fucking *demonstrate*. Information wants to be free. You just kinda—" Jacob did a thing with his tongue. She remembered the last time his tongue did that on the small of her back.

"She wants us to beg," said Jacob.

Luke smiled. Jacob smiled. They put their hands together.

"You want us on our knees?"

"That'd be nice," spat Avery. "No, don't—"

She turned eleven shades of purple as they both kicked their chairs back and got on their knees.

"Please have a threesome with us?" Jacob mouthed, no sound—but they'd both done a semester of sign language and he knew she could read his lips. Avery looked around desperately to see if there were any deaf people around.

"No! Sit the fuck down!" Avery.

"Please?" This time, Jacob, in a moan.

"Sit! Sit! Sit! No, don't—"

"Only if you agree to—" Luke.

"—even fucking say it." Avery. "*Sit*," she snapped. She was actually getting pissed, or at least she hoped they thought so. Inside, she was glowing.

They both sat down politely. The brunch crowd was glancing over, smiling; it was San Francisco, so shit like this happened daily—on a Sunday, every *hour*.

They sipped mimosas in silence; the waitress brought the check.

"Are we gonna do this?" she finally asked.

The two men looked at each other.

Jake made his *chaw!* sound.

Luke shrugged and nodded.

Avery took a deep breath. "My place?" she asked.

Luke shrugged. "It's close," he said.

"Sounds good," said Jacob.

"Yeah," said Luke. "And let's make it quick. I'm fuckin' horny."

Jacob guffawed.

"It's the shirt!" they both howled simultaneously, and fist-bumped.

Good Christ, thought Avery. *What have I done?*

She breathed three times, slammed her last mimosa, and sprinted for the door.

Under the circumstances, she figured, her two boyfriends could split the check.

It was only a few moments before they joined her on Fifth Street, but it felt like hours. She stood there, heat pulsing through her body; she wanted badly to back out, but now that she'd gotten them to agree to it, the deed felt like it was done—without an item of clothing ever being dropped.

Fifth Street was busy. Two dykes made out across the way. A guy passed in front of her and dropped his gaze; she crossed her arms in front of her. Was this actually happening?

Jacob and Luke came out of the restaurant, Jacob tucking cash into his wallet. They looked her up and down and smiled.

Jacob turned to Luke. "Dude, I'm not holding your hand."

Avery made a disgusted noise. She took one hand each, and the three of them formed a line across the sidewalk walking toward Avery's place.

Had she been a little less drunk, she might have had further second thoughts—which wouldn't have done anybody any good. When Luke broke up with her—he "needed some space," same old bullshit line every guy used—she'd resolved to be more experimental. No more monogamy. No more jumping into relationships. Dating was awesome. Fuckbuddies were cool. Casual sex was even better. Jacob had fallen somewhere at the confluence of all those categories: sex on the first date, sex on the second date, repeat ad infinitum. It had stopped being casual sex when they'd started planning sex weekends together, and she'd figured they would need to have The Talk when Luke came blasting back into her life, apologizing for being a dipshit—just what every woman wants to hear, right? She'd gone right back to bed with him, and the sex had proven far better than before; apparently he'd learned a lot in three months of being single. Avery found herself in an arrangement suspended between a love triangle, dedicated polyamory and negotiated sluttiness. Jacob didn't seem to mind. Luke was slightly more possessive, but Avery'd put her foot down: no relationships as such; no monogamy. She didn't want things to get complicated.

So how was it she was holding two guys' hands, walking them back to her apartment, about to fuck them both?

The definition of complicated.

But then, it wasn't like she hadn't planned it out a million times in her fantasies. In fact, when she'd heard Luke's voice on the phone, she'd had three thoughts. The first was *He's dialed a wrong number.* The second was, *Luke and Jacob = Threesome.*

The third thought was so filthy and distracting she'd barely heard a word Luke had said for the first half minute of his apology.

She was a very naughty girl.

"How do we do this?" asked Avery. Luke and Jacob stood on opposite ends of her, in the corners of her small living room. Her skin felt electric. It seemed to repulse them both; they repulsed each other, forming some weird fucking science experiment triangle. She felt breathlessly suspended between the two of them. Her back was to Jacob; her front was to Luke. She felt desperately asthmatic, locked in desperate breathless anticipation. She felt like she was having a panic attack. She blushed deep, her face hot, as Luke looked from her eyes to her tits.

Neither man said anything.

"How do we do this?" she repeated.

"You're the expert," said Jacob.

He had stolen up behind her, six feet plus of surfer dude towering over Avery's five-ish feet. He took hold of her waist, big hands resting gently on her hips. She trembled. He moved nearer, till his muscled body grazed her shoulder blades and buttocks. His thumbs traced the outline of her thong, visible above the too-low waistband of her jeans.

Luke crept closer, smiling enigmatically. Jacob's hands went up under Avery's soft, tight cotton sweater.

"Expert?" she moaned softly. "How big a slut do you think I am?"

"Not as big as you'll be in an hour," said Jacob.

Jacob's hands went smoothly north. At first she thought he was just cupping her tits—then the shawl collar blinded her, as Jacob lifted it neatly over her head.

"Oh god," she said nervously, her words muffled. She obediently put her arms up, letting him take off her sweater. Jacob tossed it on the couch. Luke moved closer.

"You're wearing my favorite bra," he said.

She could *feel* Jacob smirk behind her.

"Nice one, isn't it? She always wears it when she knows she's gonna get laid."

"Are you two enjoying yourselves?" she asked.

Behind her, Jacob got hold of her hands and gently held them behind her.

"Now I am," he said, kissing her neck.

Avery stiffened; his lips on her neck combined with him sort of half-pinning her arms made her so fucking hot she couldn't stand it. She sank into the sensation of Jacob kissing her as Luke moved in closer and looked her in the eyes. He reached for the clasp of her favorite bra—the thing was notoriously difficult to undo. Luke got it on the first try; Jacob let go of her hand to help Luke take it off of her, then reached down to unbutton her jeans.

The zipper stumped him, so Luke nudged Jacob's fingers out of the way and pulled the zipper down. Avery could almost feel the sizzling energy from where their hands touched. Two straight guys partnering up to undress the girl they were both about to fuck; it was freaky for them. That was so fucking hot.

As Luke took over pants duty, Jacob moved his hands up to Avery's tits; her eyes rolled back as he started gently working the nipples.

Luke lowered himself to his knees. He pulled Avery's tight jeans down her thighs with some difficulty, peeling the tight fabric away—fuck, had she really worn those out in public? As he did, Jacob tipped her head back and kissed her, hard, his tongue easing into her mouth while his hands began to work her nipples.

She kicked off her wedge-heeled mules and let Luke lovingly ease her jeans over her feet; as she stepped out of them, she felt his tongue tracing its way up her thigh. Surprised, she squirmed a little, which put her more firmly in Jacob's grasp. His big arms around her, he pinched her nipples more firmly, following the rhythms of her body. She writhed between them, feeling suddenly awkward. Jacob never let up kissing her deeply, and he never stopped working her nipples, building the pressure quickly until she was trembling with the intensity. Luke got hold of her slim, slutty thong and pulled it smoothly down her thighs. It was soaked.

How they made it to the futon, she'd never understand. It just sort of happened. Her two boys picked her up bodily, Jacob with his arms beneath her shoulders and his hands on her waist; Luke with his palms across her buttocks, arms supporting her thighs. She felt like she was flying. As they settled her into Jacob's lap, his hard-on pressed against her back. Luke took her panties off.

She let him take them, feeling a slight wave of panic as they slipped over her ankles and she was *naked*; she felt it acutely. Naked, pinned between two hot guys. She knew this simply couldn't be happening—but here she was, naked between the two guys she was fucking. The two guys she was *about* to fuck. If she'd stopped to think for a moment, or been less buzzed, she never would have let it happen—thank god for fucking mimosas, she'd tell herself later.

Luke spread her legs. He bent down low; his tongue worked up over her thighs, nearing her cunt.

Before he could reach it, Jacob's hand slid down and across Avery's flat, tattooed belly and between her smooth-shaved thighs. Her lips, too, were smooth; she'd shaved for the occasion. In fact, she'd taken to shaving almost always; it vastly improved her life's ratio of cunnilingus to fellatio, especially when Luke was around.

"You like her shaved?" purred Jacob in her ear as he caressed her smooth-soft lips and found her clit.

"I fucking *love* her shaved," Luke answered, his breath against her cunt. "Like, fucking love."

"Me, too," said Jacob. "It's a guy thing."

Luke lowered his face between Avery's thighs and planted his mouth hard against her vulva. His tongue went sliding across Jacob's fingers; Avery could feel the pressure of Jacob's hand on her clit and the caress of Luke's tongue gliding over her pussy lips. They changed places and Jacob's fingers eased inside her, stretching her tight, wet cunt gently while Luke began to lick her clit. Luke had always been a consummate pussy-hound—making up for a somewhat sloppy technique with the fact that every lick was totally his gig—not for her pleasure. Most guys were willing, sometimes even eager. With Luke? He thought of little else. And when it came to technique, a loose-lipped, free-form style usually got the job done.

It also meant he wasn't that careful about where his face was in relation to Jacob's hand.

For a second, Avery thought Jacob was caressing his face.

Fuck, that was fucking pervy. *What if*—she started thinking; then, *Fuck it. That's not gonna happen. Unless*—

The phrase was in her mouth before she could stop it: "Are you gonna kiss?"

"Probably not," said Jacob.

Luke shook his head; it sent a shiver through her clit.

"I'd kinda like it if you did," she blurted.

"'Cause you're a perv," said Jacob, matter-of-factly.

It was true. A shameless fag hag since adolescence, Avery got instantly wet whenever she thought of two guys doing it. The fact that she'd historically only ever slept with utterly straight dudes had been one of the tragedies of her life thus far.

But that wasn't why she'd figured it was time to make a play for a threesome with Jacob and Luke. When she'd hatched her half-baked plan, she hadn't thought for a second Jacob and Luke would obediently augment her turn-on by touching each other; in fact, she'd completely dismissed the possibility.

But Jacob did not remove his hand from Luke's face. It looked fucking *hot*. She might have been prejudiced, sure, since Luke's expert tongue was working her clit faster and faster as his hands reached up for her buttocks and the small of her back—

"Not there, dude. *Here*." With his free hand, which a moment before had been pinching Avery's nipples, Jacob took Luke's hand and guided it up the curve of her buttocks, past her hips, to the place—

"Oh fucking Jesus!" she cried as Jacob's firm guiding hand put Luke's fingers right where Jacob loved to kiss her.

"See? It's special."

Luke's face came up from between her legs; he grinned salaciously.

"Nice!"

Experimentally, he glided his fingertips in circles around That Fucking Spot, and Avery twisted.

"No, don't—" she gasped.

"No, don't?" asked Luke.

"Or no don't stop?" asked Jacob.

Luke's fingers tickled her there; she twisted, writhed, cried out; Luke's face descended between her legs again; he started licking her rhythmically as he caressed; it sent uneven spasms of tickling pleasure through her, but Luke wasn't nearly as practiced at it as Jacob. Once Jacob had spent an hour licking there—she had basically cum, or something like it. Luke was doing a damn fine job; her eyes rolled way back into her head and she shivered, gently humping her body up against him. But he wasn't the expert.

She felt Jacob's hand at That Fucking Spot: big, strong, heavy. "Do that thing with her feet," he said. "I'll take over with her back."

"Oh, fuck, fuck—fuck fuck fuck," she thundered. "No. No please—" She didn't know what she was saying; she writhed spasmodically between them.

Jacob turned her slightly, getting on his knees on the couch behind her, and spreading her legs so that Luke could get more firmly between her thighs. Jacob grabbed her hair. He arched her back. Jacob put his other hand down at That Spot— caressing, while pulling her hair gently, while biting her neck, gnawing, sucking, while Luke put his tongue on her clit, while Luke put his lips around the upper swell of her cunt lips, and did that *thing* he did; she'd never understand it—it was like a suck and a slurp, with a pressure somewhere no other guy could ever fucking find—and as he worked her clit Luke took her feet, one in each hand; he pushed them up to tip her vulva back at just the right angle, and each thumb found That Other Spot in the balls of her feet—

Avery screamed at the top of her lungs.

"Bad scream or good scream?" asked Jacob.

She made a "Gaaah!" sound, writhing back and forth.

"Good scream?"

"Gaah!"

"Bad scream."

"Gaaaah," she howled, and clawed at his thighs. She shut her eyes tight, the movements of her body going fucking *crazy*. If she hadn't been pinned between two humans vastly bigger than she, she would have spazzed her way across the fucking living room, and probably poured out the window to slop onto Fifth Street. As it was, she was helpless between them—as they played her like an instrument, two virtuosos playing in different keys.

"Good scream," sighed Jacob. Avery's back arched; her belly undulated; her thighs shook; her head rolled against the tight hard grip of Jacob's hand in her hair; they kept going. They just wouldn't stop. Neither guy would let up. They worked every fucking erogenous zone she'd ever known she had, and a few she'd forgotten about, minus the two she could reach with her hands—which she started to do, totally shameless, planting her hands on her tits and working her nipples hard, pinching, prodding, squeezing, digging her fingernails into her flesh as she mounted toward—

"Orgasm," said Jacob, matter-of-factly. "Our girl's about to have an orgasm," said Jacob.

"*Our* girl?" said Luke, his voice thrumming through her pubic bone.

"Our *girl*," said Jacob emphatically. He stopped gnawing on the back of her neck and tucked her upper body firmly into his arms, still holding his hair.

Then he kissed her. His tongue went in deep, thick and wet, stifling her moans as she mauled her own tits like a maddened little vixen. His mouth came off of hers with a big wet snap of spit, and she lapped at it, teeth working violently like she couldn't get enough of him—them—of herself. Of fucking everything. She was crazed.

"Cum for us," purred Jacob, one hand pulling at her hair,

the other gently caressing her face. Her eyes popped open wide and that was what did it; she'd looked into his eyes as she'd climaxed before—as creepy and Tantra as that sounds—but never like *this*. She came so hard she felt her fillings crack.

And neither boy had ever really heard her *scream* before. In fact, no human ever had; no creature had, except her cat. Which was not as dirty as it sounded; that is to say, when she came as hard as she came that day, it was usually vibrator-driven after hours of porn—and no one was listening, because Avery was always too embarrassed to seriously let go.

But this time, people were listening; two people, and probably the neighbors; possibly much of this city block and some of the next. She screamed anyway, at the top of her lungs, thrashing wildly back and forth until she had to push Luke's face away and shut her thighs and beg them, "Stop, stop, stop, stop, stop!"

"Really stop this time?" asked Jacob.

"Uh," she said, and clutched him close. Luke took a seat on the couch, with her feet in his lap; she shot him a warning look and he grinned.

"So, whuddaya say, dude?" It was Jacob: The cheeky one.

She was so brain-dead from screaming and coming that she didn't follow the innuendo, until after it was over. Even as Luke shot Jacob a sketchball look, she just lay there gaping and drooling.

"She said it'd really turn her on," said Jacob.

Luke sighed.

"Weird," he said. "Fucking weird."

Jacob eased himself out from under her; he tucked pillows under her back and leaned way over toward Luke.

"Let's try not to make it too gay," said Jacob, as he came in for the kiss.

And then his mouth was hard on Luke's—not even tentative; not a girl-kiss; not even a girls-while-their-boyfriends-are-watching kiss. Just a kiss; a fucking open-mouthed, lots-of-tongue kind of kiss. And it lasted.

When their mouths came apart, there was spit. There was *spit*. Avery moaned.

Both boys looked at her, smiled, turned back; they kissed again, deep again, and Avery watched, gape-mouthed, moaning, wide-eyed.

It just came out of her mouth before she could stop it—in a low, soft, rapturous moan, rich with promise.

"Oh my god. Thank you. *Thank* you!"

They finished kissing and high-fived.

One of them said, "Let's go to bed," and that was good enough for her.

REMINDER

Jeremy Edwards

The first time Deborah brought Angie home with her, it was not in the flesh, but as a phenomenon; a discussion topic; a *something to share*.

"I had a reminder today," she confided in Paul, when they were snuggling on the couch after dinner, each with a book at hand but neither actually reading.

"A reminder? Of what?"

"A reminder that I'm attracted to women sometimes." She knew Paul understood, had always understood.

"Ah," he replied, with a relaxed cheerfulness. He gave her knee a sexy little love-squeeze.

"Gonna do anything about it?" he said after a moment.

He stroked her shoulder now, and she felt everything in his fingertips—his support, his arousal, his unconditional but never smothering love. She felt her security and her freedom, between which things she was never forced to choose.

"Well, I probably won't see her again. She was just a stranger in the supermarket. And at the credit union."

"You saw her both places?"

"Yeah. So I guess that means the odds of running into her again are that much slimmer."

"Actually, that's a common fallacy." Paul had studied statistics more recently than Deborah. "Seeing her twice in one outing doesn't mean your chances of seeing her in the future are reduced." He warmed to his theme. "In fact, if we hypothesize that she regularly uses *both* the same supermarket and the same bank that we do, this increases the chances of a future sighting, compared to a scenario where you'd seen her only one place or the other."

"This is true. Still, I'm not going to get my hopes up. As far as I'm concerned, she's just a reminder."

"It's nice to have reminders, isn't it?" said Paul.

"Yes, it *is* nice," said Deborah, cuddling up closer to her husband.

"Lucky stranger in the supermarket," Paul whispered seductively, "getting into your pants like this, without even knowing it."

His voice in her ear awakened Deborah's erogenous zones from head to toe, the way streetlamps lit up one after another at dusk. "Right now I want *you* in my pants," she whispered back.

She pivoted on the couch, swinging a leg up to bring the crotch of her jeans in contact with his knee. She rubbed herself against him, slowly but intensely, as she described the stranger in the supermarket.

Normally, Paul was the one to run most of the errands. He had the time for it, and the taste for it. Moreover, he was the one who was organized enough to do them promptly and efficiently. Deb was a go-getter, an inspired and energetic entrepreneur, but keeping track of things was *not* her forte. As a result of their division of labor, Deb had half forgotten what running errands was like.

For example, she'd forgotten that when you ran errands,

you saw *people*. Some of them attractive. Oh, she knew Paul very much enjoyed that aspect of the process—seeing the types of women that appealed to him cross his field of vision while he bustled around town. It was no secret—and no threat. She cheered him on in his appreciation for them. But she'd forgotten that she herself was in line for the same fringe benefits, when she occasionally took a turn at the shopping. Typically, it was the thirtysomething boys her eyes registered—her male peers—though only the more interesting ones got her attention.

But, as she'd related to Paul, this vivacious, not-quite-boyish-figured female peer had been a reminder, not just that errands meant attractive people, but that Deborah liked girls too. Deborah was a bisexual who could go months at a time thinking only of men—her man, the TV and movie stars she fancied, the delicious guys she met sometimes in her work life. But then, all of a sudden, she'd be bowled over by the feminine. Last time it had been during an autumn warm spell, when she'd taken a shortcut across the campus between afternoon meetings downtown, only to find her clit skipping with glee over a landscape of quietly frolicking college girls with cute knees and bangs. These women, too, had been welcome reminders, as Deborah rushed past them.

This time, she couldn't believe her luck in encountering that face and those legs and that ass twice in one day. First she'd noticed the woman—*noticed* was an understatement—in line at the credit union. The radiant, impish face had smiled at Deborah while they each awaited a teller; then the perky little behind in the berry-colored denim shorts, and the smooth, muscular legs proud beneath them, had stridden alluringly forward when it was the woman's turn at the counter.

Thirty minutes later, at the supermarket, Deborah had come

to a full stop, both physically and psychologically, when her hitherto-grocery-scanning gaze suddenly focused on the woman ahead of her, who had halted her cart midway down the aisle. There was no mistaking that jumbled blonde-and-brown sweep of hair, halfway between elfin and hippie, or those bright raspberry-red shorts.

Sensing Deborah's need to pass by, the woman scurried to one side with a brief ass-wiggle—clearly more wiggle than was strictly necessary for the maneuver, as emphasized by the way she grinned back over her shoulder, as if to say, not merely, *Can you get by now?* but also, *Did you notice how yummy I am? Yes, and yes*, thought Deborah.

They crossed paths one last time five minutes later, when the woman turned a corner into the aisle Deb was just leaving, pausing for a fraction of a second to smile again at Deb before bopping off on her way. Her eyes were large, her gaze joyful and curious.

Packed into the car with her groceries, Deborah wished she could spend the next twenty minutes masturbating instead of driving. All she could think about was how she longed to kiss that woman at the crotch of her raspberry shorts . . . then pull them down, tickle her thighs, and watch a wet spot of excitement appear at the gusset of her undies. She longed to bury her nose and mouth between those concisely round and cajoling buttocks, feasting on the cheeks, then slip farther down to dine on a succulent pussy. She longed to see that face blossom into even greater joy with Deb's fingers working to pleasure her.

She drove home, her bottom squirming on the seat every bit of the way.

Despite her resolve not to get her hopes up, Deb fantasized about encountering the woman all over town, from the post

office to the garden-supply store to the wine shop—places she
didn't even usually go, leaving it to Paul. Then the daydreams
became more exotic, taking Deborah to locations she'd hardly
ever seen, at the periphery of the town: A boathouse. A hot-
air-balloon launch. A Ferris wheel. With no conscious direction
on Deborah's part, the visions had rippled out from suburban
reality to semi-magical playlands—celebrating their own status
as fantasies, as scenarios removed from the here and now. In
her imagination, these whimsical venues were united by their
purpose of landing Deb in the company of that one specific
stranger, and from there it was a quick transition to the X-rated
fantasy sequences that followed.

It was six weeks before Deborah ran errands again. This time
it was not at the supermarket, nor at the credit union, that she
spotted Angie (as the crisp, elegant lettering on a name tag now
described her); she was stocking ink cartridges at the computer
store. Their eyes met in recognition, and Angie's already bright
face lit up further.

Now Deborah knew where to find her.

Paul usually dropped by the computer store once a week, for
one thing or another. All Deborah had to do was volunteer to
relieve him of that particular errand, until further notice. Of
course, she told him the reason.

Once this arrangement was in place, Deb suspected Paul
was making a point of ensuring there was always at least one
computer-related item on the household shopping list, so she
would never miss a week. On one occasion he crossed off the
items she'd just purchased and immediately wrote down a new
one, without even stepping away from the refrigerator door, his
confident hand gliding purposefully over the list. On another
occasion he added *Look at your friend's ass* below *USB cable
for scanner,* as a separate item.

On Deb's fourth visit to the computer store, she heard Angie speak.

"What's up, Alexandra?" she said as another employee approached her.

"Hey, Angie. Just wanted to tell you I'll be covering the copy center for a bit, while Bob does his thing in the back office."

"Oh. I didn't realize Bob was a sexual contortionist," Angie deadpanned.

Alexandra squealed with delight, then, looking guiltily around, she hissed a *"Stop!"* at her colleague before bursting out anew with giggles.

"Anyway, it's nice of you to pitch in—so he can make both ends meet."

Alexandra, now helpless with laughter, disappeared into a different aisle, shielding her face with a clipboard so as not to catch Angie's eye again.

It seemed too good to be true that Angie had, on top of everything else, a fast and naughty wit; and yet Deborah felt she had expected it from the first time she saw the sparkle in the woman's face.

It was on the sixth visit that Angie spoke to *her.*

"Hi, gorgeous," she said with an easy familiarity, nearly making Deborah believe they'd known each other forever. This was not the presumptuous "Hi, gorgeous" of the typical boundary-crossing stranger. No, Angie's "Hi, gorgeous" managed to present itself as casual, appropriate, and pressure free, but with a pretty doorknob on it for Deb to use if she wanted to make more of it.

This was exactly what she did want.

"Hello, yourself," she replied to Angie, smiling appreciatively over her trembles and hoping the word *yourself* was coming through complete with its subtext, *You're pretty damn adorable.*

Angie touched Deborah's arm as she looked directly in her eyes to repurpose the standard customer-service sound bite: "Let me know if you need anything."

So, yes, the messages back and forth had been efficiently received, and Deborah readied herself for what she needed to say next. In this moment, they had quickly leaped from "friendly flirting" to "flirting with serious intent," and Deborah would never engage in the latter without coming clean about her situation.

"Thank you," she began. Now it was she who reached out to touch the other woman's elbow, as they stood there alone in the ink-cartridge aisle.

This was always the hard part. "I should tell you that I'm married," she said quietly. "Very, very happily married." She cleared her throat, working through the nervous dryness. "But I liked it very much when you called me 'gorgeous'—and I also happen to know that my husband would applaud your calling me 'gorgeous.'" She returned her hand to Angie's elbow, and left it there this time.

"Good to know," Angie said softly, but with a hot twinkle. "And what else would your husband applaud?"

Deborah exhaled. Sometimes it wasn't so hard, after all. "Suppose we go home later and find out?"

They made their plans, and in her flush of excitement Deborah knocked a sale display of pens over as she spun around to leave.

"Sorry!" she winced. "Can't take me anywhere, I guess."

Angie laughed as she squatted suggestively in her shorts, straddling the fallen pen-holder to gather up the wayward merchandise. "Oh, sweetheart, I bet there are at least one or two places you can be taken."

When Deb picked Angie up at her house that evening, the

pixie had changed from her shorts and computer-store T-shirt into a thin black jersey and a long, clinging print skirt. Exquisite nipple peaks atop the small rounds of her breasts spoke to the absence of a bra.

Playful conversation flowed naturally in the car. Deb also discovered that the close quarters of the coupe meant she could smell the fresh hungry aroma of Angie's pussy. Deb relished the progression: from seeing Angie, to hearing her, to touching her, she had segued to smelling her, with tasting and much more touching and seeing and hearing inevitably to follow.

Paul, having heard the engine in the driveway, greeted them right in the foyer, the eager caramel warmth in his eyes making his tidy chestnut beard look a shade lighter.

Angie half shouted an extroverted hello before the door was even closed.

"Welcome," said Paul. "Deb phoned and told me she'd be bringing home a friend. You're obviously the Angie whereof she speaks."

Deborah embraced him as she elaborated. "Actually, I phoned and told him that Angie, the hottie I'd been babbling about for weeks, had consented to cross our threshold. Like I explained, Paul and I have no secrets."

"Excellent," said Angie, her tone a parody of ceremoniousness. "I shall share my secret as well. Paul, it is my secret intention to undress this Deborah whereof we speak at the earliest opportunity."

"A commendable idea," said Paul, with a stiff, comical little bow, which he instantly followed up with Grouchoesque eyebrow business. "Did you have a particular room in mind?"

Deborah beamed while Paul chattered on amiably. "Personally, I like to undress Deborah in our bedroom, but I might also recommend the living room." He fondled his wife's bottom.

"There's a couch in there that it's rather pleasant to watch her sink into."

Angie added her own hand to Deborah's rear, taking the buttock her husband wasn't busy caressing. She cupped her other hand over Deb's fly.

She winked at Paul, then squirreled her left hand through Deb's crotch from behind, to clasp her around the thigh. Paul, quick on the uptake, mirrored the move from his side, and together they hoisted Deb and carried her, giggling, to the living-room sofa. Paul stepped aside as Deborah sank into the couch, letting Angie stand over her.

Angie turned in profile to adjust the cushion under Deb's shoulders. Seeing that Deb was ogling her ass, she grinned and settled her skirt farther down her hips, so as to expose roughly a third of her bottom for her playmate. The compact cheeks flared enthusiastically out from the abbreviated smirk of asscrack, and Deborah reached up deliriously to tickle the inviting crevice. It was apparent now that Angie's nonexistent bra formed a matched set with her nonexistent panties. No wonder her feminine scent had been so immediate in the car, Deb thought.

Deborah's panties were so moist they seemed to be sticking to her jeans. This sensation, though delectably raunchy, was a fleeting one, as Angie acted fast to peel her host nude from the waist down. The guest then took some time kissing and sucking the host's toes.

Paul stood in the background. Though Deborah's eyes took the line of Angie's hair, back, and bottom—which now wiggled happily in the air as Angie knelt atop sofa cushions—she could sense her husband's attention.

A gentle dive forward, and Angie had covered Deborah with her body. She dotted Deb's face with kisses and established sensuous handholds on Deb's breasts, which tingled gratefully

through a bra and a fitted blouse. Deb welcomed Angie's asser-
tiveness with all this, and her intellect just had time to articulate
relief that she didn't have to break the ice before her conscious-
ness skittered off into more primal avenues. She managed to
answer Angie's grip with handholds of her own on the waistband of Angie's derriere-previewing skirt, pushing the fabric
down Angie's thighs until she was at the extent of her reach,
then letting Angie finish the task.

Their naked pussies now ground their friendship freely at the
sofa's midpoint, the damp furs of the two muffs blending and
inter-tickling. Angie's hands continued to nurture Deb's breasts,
and Deborah's fingers ran wildly up and down the crack of the
other woman's behind, making the cheeks vibrate around them.

Breasts freighted themselves with sensitivity as tops came
off. Angie humped Deb more vigorously and suckled her, while
Deb twisted Angie's nipples and played indefatigably with her
ass. The two women pressed and groped and teased each other
into a fragrant, slippery frenzy.

Paul had settled down on the floor by the couch, where he
ducked the frequent involuntary kicks of assorted pleasure-
crazed legs. It penetrated Deb's awareness that he could either
remain a contented observer . . . or become a grateful participant.

"I want Paul to make me come," she panted impulsively into
Angie's mouth.

"Fuck, yes," Angie returned. "Make us come, Paul, make us
fucking come."

Two well-engorged clits. Two deftly operated male forefin-
gers.

Two couch-rocking orgasms.

Two women kissing each other's faces in ecstasy and filling
the house with their laughing, crying satiation.

* * *

They made it a weekly thing, with Angie crossing their threshold every Friday at 7:00 PM Meanwhile, at midweek, Paul had resumed the computer-store shopping runs, always returning with comradely reports of kidding around with Angie, and bearing the cheerful messenger's burden of ornately specific instructions like, "Give your lovely wife a slow-motion wet tonguing down the length of her slit for me."

"You don't feel that my Angie time is impoverishing *our* time, right?" Deborah lifted her head up from Paul's naked lap to double-check, one Thursday.

Paul chuckled reassuringly. "Au contraire, muffin."

She shuddered with arousal as he dispatched the thought with a nice slap to her rump.

One Monday, Deborah rediscovered with a shock the plans she'd made months earlier—then forgotten—for two back-to-back weekends away with Paul, to visit different family members. The first trip was scheduled for the coming Friday.

That night, she lost sleep over how to break it to Angie that they weren't on for their usual Friday-night fun, either this week or the following—and that inviting her over on another weeknight was out of the question as well, because of Deb's full calendar of meetings.

They'd even had a discussion last Friday about which new positions they wanted to try the next week, poring over a pictorial lesbian-sex guide in a nude three-sided committee, with Paul's erection pointing involuntarily to his own favorite diagrams.

"I'm sure it won't be a big deal," said Paul on Tuesday morning.

"I don't know, Paul. She might really be upset. She might even think I'm lying about the schedule conflicts. Oh, it would just kill me if she thought that."

He made another attempt. "But it could have happened to anyone."

"No, it couldn't have," sniffed Deborah. "One spaced weekend commitment, maybe. But *two in a row?* That's the kind of thing that only happens to me."

"Well, I love you."

Bingo. Eventually, Paul always found the right thing to say.

Deborah went to the computer store that afternoon.

"What's wrong, gorgeous?" As she'd shown on the very first occasion they'd conversed, Angie was adept at reading Deb's feelings.

Deb explained, holding back tears, about the conflicts on Friday the fifteenth and Friday the twenty-second.

Angie took her hand. "Well, all I can say is you're going to have one horny girlfriend waiting for you on Friday the twenty-ninth. Don't be surprised if you find me camped out on your doorstep with my panties halfway down."

Angie chuckled at her own hyperbole, and Deb guffawed with amusement and relief, even as her clit danced at the image Angie had conjured up.

"Oh, come on, babe—I bet you have some other friends you can play with while we're gone." Angie had never expressly said that, but she'd hinted at it. Now she licked her lips mischievously at the supposition, and Deborah had a beautiful vision of Angie sprawling naked on a carpet with Alexandra.

Deborah turned serious again. "Are you sure it's okay? I'm so sorry about this, sweetie."

Angie touched her cheek, then subtly grazed a nipple before resting her hand on Deb's waist. "Never worry."

During the drive home two weeks later, Deborah asked herself if she was in love with Angie.

She certainly didn't love Angie the way she loved Paul—and she knew she never would. She could never, for instance, imagine offering Angie that exuberant, spontaneous expression of total devotion whereby she'd suddenly seize Paul around the middle, squeeze him and French-kiss him, and then continue going about her business, with no words exchanged.

But she could envision a label that said *love*, in smaller and different lettering from the love she shared with Paul, being applied to Angie before long—perhaps, she thought to herself with a grin, the same lettering used on Angie's name tag.

Love. Maybe Deborah wasn't ready yet to inhabit that emotion with respect to her woman friend, but at least she could get near it.

Would that be okay? Would Angie want Deborah to love her more than Deborah could? Or to love her *less* than Deborah would? All of a sudden, the possibilities seemed intimidating.

And then she remembered Angie's face in the ink-cartridge aisle: *"Never worry."*

"Never worry," Deborah echoed aloud, thereby rousing Paul from a concurrent reverie.

"Hmm?" He blinked at her inquiringly.

Deborah blushed at her accidental utterance, but did not regret it. "I was giving myself a little pep talk. You know . . . a reminder."

Paul smiled but said nothing, and the space felt just right.

SLEEPER CAR

Max Lagos

Chris stared out the window, starting his sixth continuous hour. The landscape flashing by had lost his interest somewhere around Fargo, North Dakota, and now the barren fields were just numbing his brain.

One of the benefits to traveling for work was the private roomette Chris occupied on the westbound train. He could have been in Seattle days ago if he had been willing to go anywhere near an airport, but he wasn't.

So it was the Amtrak Empire Builder line for him, servicing such exotic locales as Portage, Wisconsin, and Cut Bank, Montana. Chris had never really understood the word *alone* before traveling by himself. Not that he was a particularly social guy anyway, but being tucked away in his private room made him feel much more, well, alone.

Even so, Chris considered canceling his reservations in the dining car and having dinner in his room. But the boredom was getting to him, and he needed to stretch his legs.

"Everyone holding a six-fifteen dinner reservation, please make your way to the dining car," a voice echoed from the overhead speaker. Chris staggered from his room toward the dining car, rhythmically slamming his shoulders on the walls in the narrow corridor as the train rocked back and forth.

"Dinner tonight is by community seating." The hostess smiled. "Please have a seat with this lovely couple here."

Oh, crap, Chris thought. *Stuck with some backwoods yokels, trying to avoid small talk and eye contact. I gotta eat fast and get out of here.* He slid into the booth and smiled his best fake smile at his dinner companions.

"Hi, what's your name?" the girl asked.

"Chris."

"Hi, Chris. I'm Wendy, and this is Martin. Where are you going?"

"Seattle. You?"

"Us too! It's our honeymoon," Wendy gushed, smiling lovingly at Martin. They leaned forward and pressed their lips together, Martin's tongue roughly and rather lewdly penetrating his wife's mouth. Chris felt a sudden pressure against his zipper as his cock responded to the other man's unintentional voyeurism. He looked down at his menu to regain his composure.

"Congratulations . . ." Chris mumbled before the conversation was interrupted by Mary, the hostess, bringing a fourth person to their table. Mr. Jenkins, as everyone learned over their main course, was a ninety-year-old retired pharmacist, with ninety years of boring stories to prove it.

"So, Chris," Wendy piped in, breaking a stimulating monologue about the benefits of using name-brand medications instead of generic brands. "Are you gay?"

Mr. Jenkins was mid-swallow of coffee and choked the hot liquid down.

"Why do you ask?" Chris replied, looking into Wendy's laughing eyes. A quick check of Martin's revealed the other man's interest in the answer as well.

"Well, partially to make Mr. Jenkins shoot coffee out his nose. But mostly because I am getting a feeling from you, and I can't really figure out what it is."

"Actually, I'm bi. I usually don't give off gay vibes though. Hmm, maybe I'm not as far in the closet as I thought I was."

Martin laughed. "No, more likely because my lovely wife is very sensitive to anything dirty." Martin squeezed his wife's hand with a smile. "She's a true slut." The two young men locked eyes across the table, Chris catching a flicker of something decidedly lusty.

"Well, excuse me," Mr. Jenkins managed through his fluster. Standing and practically running from the car, he muttered something about needing a nap and disappeared.

"Well it's about time he left, boring old fart," Wendy laughed. "So, Chris, we have been fucking like rabbits since we left Chicago." She leaned forward conspiratorially. "We gave our attendant twenty bucks to leave our bed down and leave us alone."

"Cool." Chris took another drink of his Sierra Mist and let his mind wander to his last sexual encounter. It had been so long ago, most of the details were forgotten. "I haven't gotten laid in weeks. Once you've been married longer, you'll know what I mean."

"Aww, poor baby." Wendy reached across and held Chris's hand. "Why don't you come back to our bedroom and fuck with us?"

Chris just looked at her blankly for a second. But only for a second. With a laugh, he said, "Sure, off we go then." To his great surprise, his companions started to slide from the booth.

Realizing they were serious and this was getting close to the actual fulfilling of his greatest fantasy, Chris practically dove from the booth. Wendy led the two men into the next car, the same one Chris's little room was in. With a dramatic flourish, Wendy slid the door open. "Get in there, bitches. Mama needs to be serviced."

Chris fell onto the disheveled mattress, Martin practically jumping in on top of him. His weight pressed Chris deep into the bed as their mouths found each other. Chris sighed inwardly, feeling Martin's stubble against his cheeks and chin. It had been three years since Rob had dumped him on Valentine's Day, and Chris hadn't felt another man's lips since.

"Holy fuck, guys! Wait for me!" Wendy laughed, pulling off her clothes. Martin broke contact, playfully tugging on Chris's lower lip with his teeth. He nipped and sucked on his wife's offered neck, hands roaming her soft body as she hurriedly made him naked as well.

Turning her focus back to their guest, Wendy climbed onto the mattress, straddling Chris's still-clothed body. Slowly crawling and sliding her moist cunt until it was inches from his mouth, she whispered, voice hoarse with lust, "Eat me."

Chris took a deep breath, inhaling her musk as Wendy lowered her wanting pussy onto his face. The first contact of her soft lips against his was like being hit by a bolt of lightning. Her cunt was sopping, and his face was awash with her essence in seconds.

Chris tried to match the rhythm of Wendy's frantic grinding against his face but it was no use. She was rubbing her sex against his lips using a beat generated in her loins that only she could follow. "Fuck, fuck, fuck . . ." Wendy panted, leaning forward against the window to steady herself.

Strong hands at his belt brought Chris's attention back

to the fact there was a third person rocking back and forth in the train's small bedroom as well. Unable to assist in any way without ending the tongue-lashing he was administering to Wendy's greedy cunt, Chris lay still as Martin opened the button on his jeans and unzipped the fly.

"Mmm," Martin moaned as he bent forward to lay his lips on the fabric-covered bulge of Chris's demanding erection. The sensation sent a deep, guttural moan from Chris's soul directly into the pussy mashed into his face, sending its mistress over the edge of orgasm.

The flood of Wendy's thick juice took Chris by surprise but not as much as his cock being pulled violently from his briefs and engulfed by Martin's hot mouth. Intense pleasure quickly overwhelmed shock as Martin sucked, licked, and nipped Chris's manhood with a talent he must have spent long hours perfecting.

Chris tried to tell him to slow down . . . he was going too fast . . . getting close to his own eruption, but the mouthful of Wendy's cunt still made him unintelligible. As she worked out her last shudders of bliss, he found himself unable to do anything but mumble and moan.

The exquisite pain of coming forced Chris's hips off the bouncing mattress and nearly knocked Wendy to the floor. Martin grasped Chris's tight ass and, holding him aloft, kept the jerking cock deep in his throat. Chris could feel Martin struggling to drink all his offering but could not slow his ejaculation any more than he could stop the speeding train he rode.

Spent, Wendy flopped to the bed on Chris's left and snuggled in close. Martin pressed his lean body against Chris's right and both rested their heads on his heaving chest, kissing like newly-weds, tender and slow.

"Holy crap," Chris moaned when he had collected himself enough to speak. "That was incredible."

Martin brought his head up and kissed Chris on the neck, nibbling at his pulsing vein. "No, that was just foreplay. But I imagine we will hit incredible sometime before Seattle."

THE BENEFIT
OF THE DOUBT

Cole Riley

The sky was darkening up, with heavy, menacing clouds. I rushed out of the apartment, forgetting my cell phone and my umbrella. There had been a series of days like this, passing in a blur, unfocused and almost meaningless. No sense fooling myself that everything was going well, because it was not.

"Where to, fella?" the cabbie asked as soon I slid into the backseat.

"Central Park West and West 100th Street," I replied.

Today was something I had dreaded. I felt like a zombie, on autopilot, and I needed to be sharp. Maybe I had been sleeping four or five hours a night. I'd been sleepwalking through the days, too tired to notice anything. Maybe that was why our triad, our Poly family, was unraveling.

The other day, Inez, a saucy Latina, pulled me into the kitchen and said, "Everything is coming down around you and you think everything's cool. Alex's doing his own thing, Kat's screwing everything not nailed down, and you're in a coma."

"And what's up with you?" I asked. The Three Musketeers plus One.

Her grip tightened on me. "I'm just waiting. Somebody's got to lead us out of this mess. It should be you. You're the sensible one, Derek."

"You're right," I said. I'd been so stressed that I'd forgotten what it felt like to be awake and alert.

With that affirmation, Inez gave me a smooch. We'd both tried to fit the monogamy mold, do that romantic thing, and be all our partner needed. What bull! Inez got married, had two kids, and divorced. Her old man and his family conspired to take away the children, flew back to the Dominican Republic, and she had not heard anything from them since.

In my case, I was engaged to a gorgeous girl who was totally into herself. She imagined she was a movie star or a supermodel. Every mirror was her pal. Every show of attention from a male was like catnip. She thrived on it; she craved it.

One weekend, I was supposed to be out of town. My Dad was sick, following another heart seizure. This was a time when my family was so supportive, so loving, so considerate. I had a kind of emergency at the job and the boss asked me to stay just that one night, and come that next day. My mother said I should stay and come out the following day. I went over to my lady's place in Hell's Kitchen, let myself in, and started fixing dinner. I knew she would be tired after a day of doing social work with the locals.

To make a long story short, I surprised my fiancée leading another man by the hand, his other digits under her dress, and his face plastered to hers in a passionate kiss.

Following a hasty retreat by her lover, we sat in the living room and calmly talked about this episode of straying. I was boiling inside.

My fiancée lit a cigarette and looked sadly at me. "I met this person. He seems nice. I want to explore a relationship with him."

I was stunned. "How long has this been going on?"

She took a series of deep breaths and frowned. "None of your business. It's like this. I don't think we can go on pretending like we're a happy couple."

"How long has this been going on?" I repeated. Suddenly I felt like a fool, and that answer was precious to me.

My fiancée exhaled a long plume of smoke, reached into her purse, and retrieved my engagement ring. I hadn't even noticed she didn't have it on. Her finely tapered fingers dropped the ring on the table and we sat staring at it as if it were a copperhead snake.

I picked up the ring, tears in my eyes, and stumbled down the stairs and out of her life. Our wedding plans stuck in my chest like a hot knife, the big church celebration with hundreds of guests, the high-priced pastor, the eager bridesmaids, and the honeymoon suite in Atlantic City. What a fool I'd been! Men don't usually notice until it's too late.

It was on one of the drunken binges that I met Inez. We were both drowning our sorrow and disappointment. After a couple of weeks, we stopped going to the bar and went on a real date instead, talking very candidly about what had just happened to us. She liked jazz concerts and movies. We went to a lot of them. I liked sport events: basketball, baseball, and football. She liked to have fun. It was through her that I discovered polyamory, the Poly Life, and one primary couple with a lover or two or three.

"I'm tired of moping, I want to have fun," Inez laughed, with her tiny gap between her front teeth like a cute schoolgirl. "Don't you want to have fun? I'm tired of mourning over people who weren't really worth the time or energy."

I smiled and nodded. Anything but this sadness. This was what happened when you took your eye off the ball. I had a tendency to let things slide until they got into a crisis.

We got an Uber ride to Astoria, Queens, where she knew of a cuddle party, a Poly social event where couples and the curious could come, learn about each other, talk shop, and even touch one another. It was delightful. Such freedom! That was when we met Kat, a curly-haired beauty with a heart-stopping figure.

At the party, Inez was immediately attracted to Kat, and soon their arms were around each other, their faces almost touching. I watched them go off into the shadows for privacy. Inez saw me following them, with a wry smile on her lips. More whispers. Kat tipped her face to my friend, inviting a kiss.

No more words, but the passion engulfed the two women. When they were half undressed, I saw their breasts were exposed, and one of Kat's was seized by Inez. She lowered her head and put her mouth on her lover's swollen nipple. I left when Inez knelt down, removed the woman's panties from under her dress, and placed her face between Kat's moist thighs. The moans coming from the dark hallway echoed in my ears.

Being polyamorous, I made room in my life for Inez and Kat, who eased right into my routine, giving me great joy with how they treated each other and me. They became lovers and more than friends. I was honored as they shared their love and desire with me, and our little family thrived, growing to a fairly lengthy revolving list of lovers. Ava, Nina, Astrid, Vicky, Cherry, Ivy, April, Luna, Jillian, Holly, and Ashley.

And then Alex, the hunky electrician, entered our lives and turned it upside down. He was totally self-involved. Sometimes I hated him for his silly demands and whims. The women loved him because he was a good fuck who would do anything for a thrill.

"Derek, I love Alex," Inez said. "With him, you know what you're getting. A booty call with frills. At least he asked for what he wanted. No guesswork. With you, I want to get to know you better, know you as a person."

I thanked her. Before Alex's arrival, everything seemed good. Then Kat started acting out. That was why we as a family were going into therapy, to keep us together, to save us.

When I got to the therapist's office, Inez and Alex were already there, chatting with the therapist, Dr. Marina Doyle. The woman, with close-cropped gray hair like Moe from the Three Stooges, was sitting with the pair. She was dressed business casual. I could see I had interrupted them in the middle of a debate over safe sex, fluid bonding, and condoms.

"Excuse me, I'm so late," I said, sitting quickly.

Alex was a little miffed. "Where's Kat? I thought she was with you. She called and said she was riding down with you."

Inez crossed her legs and sighed. Everyone was fed up with Kat's drama. She was a thrill-seeker, but sometimes a Poly family needed stability.

"We all know that Kat is screwing someone outside the group," she blurted out. "Her behavior is putting everyone at risk. Who knows what this punk is into?"

Dr. Doyle held up a hand to quiet her before she blew a fuse. "Is the group jealous of Kat? Are you jealous of her glowing with that new-lover energy?"

My brows furrowed. "That's rubbish."

"Different things can make you jealous," the doctor said. "The group has changed and it is she who has changed it. A new lover. A new situation. You see, you think polyamory will make you immune to jealousy. It does not. We're all human."

"I know the rules, but it's hard on us," Alex barked. "She

lied to us. She lied to our faces, told us she was going out with some old school friends. How can you trust someone like that?"

The doctor gave him a knowing smile. "Nobody wants to talk about relationship matters, especially when your partners think everything is all right. It's so important to talk it out rather than going off an emotional cliff. Don't tell your partners what they want to hear."

"That's what I tell them," Alex smirked. "Be up front."

I jumped into the mix. "You know, we talked about this before. You must be responsible for your decisions and actions, because what might be appropriate to you might not be that to one of the group. Like this Kat affair; if the group decides this is a wrong move, we can veto that relationship."

Inez asked the group in a loud voice, "Just who is this punk? We know nothing about him. We haven't even met him."

The doctor tried to act as mediator, speaking calmly. "And maybe that's what you need to do, meet him. I think the group sees this new lover as a threat to you, a competitor. As you folks said, you have dehumanized him, distrusted him, put him down. That's probably why Kat has resisted getting rid of him."

"But Kat doesn't want to let the group have anything to do with this dude," Alex said. "Why is she so afraid to share him with us?"

My mind flashed back to when Kat had another forbidden fling with Trevor, who she picked up in Macy's buying socks. I watched them fuck, watched him bite her slender neck while he pounded her with savage thrusts. She stared at me with sadness in her eyes. Then he came, shivering, without any concern for her. He flipped her against the wall, separated her cheeks, and went at her from the rear.

Inez was completely irate, for she was madly in love with

Kat. Her rage and disappointment underlined her betrayal and her commitment to her lover.

"Yes, she lied to everyone," she said, seething. "I'm tired of being irrational. I'm tired of being jealous. I can't make her love me. I can't force her to be loyal to me or the group. Doctor, you say be respectful, be considerate, but how can you do that when she lies all the time?"

Almost on cue, Kat, dressed in a yellow rain slicker, burst into the room, plopping down on an empty chair in the corner. I imagined she had nothing on underneath it. She appeared upset about something.

"Join us," the doctor said politely.

Kat dragged the chair just behind us, as if she knew she was the subject of conversation. She waited for the doctor to ask her why she was so late.

"Yeah, why were you late?" Inez repeated. "You knew about our meeting."

With that, Kat stood and glared at her partner. "I was doing something you should have been doing. You knew your sister, Paloma, had to go to court to testify against that scumbag doctor who almost killed her friend in the butt enhancement procedure. That girl from your old neighborhood had to be rushed to the hospital after the bastard put silicone in her ass. He injected it illegally and sealed the wounds with Krazy Glue. She almost died. Did you tell her you were going to go with her?"

"Oh damn . . ." Inez said, slumping forward.

"Nobody is concerned with what I'm going through," Kat moaned. "All I ask is that you guys talk to me. Not around me. You can talk to me about anything. All the time. Instead, you whisper and spread rumors. You, Alex, and Inez are the worst, spreading bull, relaying information. Come to me and I'll set you straight."

"What about this punk you've been screwing?" Inez asked. Alex followed up. "What did you do this time?"

"Stress makes me horny," Kat admitted. "With all of the shit I was going through in the group and at my parents', I flipped out. I got a little restless so I seduced this guy. I did him and two others without any permission from the group. I knew I did wrong. I tried to talk to Derek, but he had his own stuff going on."

I sighed and admitted she couldn't have talked to me.

"If you would have only included us, we wouldn't have felt left out or threatened," Inez said. "But you didn't. You should have introduced them to us. That's all I'm saying."

"But that doesn't mean if Inez was sleeping with one of the guys, then jealousy would go away," I countered. "Isn't that right?"

The doctor leaned back and smiled. "Jealousy is a tricky thing. For you to fight it off, you must uncover what is causing that jealousy and confront it with the truth. Tell the truth. Everybody tell the truth, even if it hurts. If you're afraid or feel insecure, then deal with it."

I amended that idea. "But the group must be the priority. I thought the concept of polyamory was to evolve, to go beyond the people we were in the old monogamous relationships. I'm committed to polyamory."

"Then be certain that your decisions, your intentions, and your actions match," the doctor said. "Don't lie to yourself. That's the worst kind of lies. Let the relationships grow organically in the group and strengthen into something lasting."

"What about me?" Kat asked pitifully. "Is the group going to put me out?"

The doctor shook her head. "I can't speak for the group, but I think another chance is in order. Don't shut down that little voice in your head that is saying to resist when you know a thing is wrong. Your head must overrule your heart sometimes. Or your loins."

Alex grinned. "I say we give Kat another chance. We've all done stupid shit. But we must follow the rules of the group. We cannot break them."

"I agree," I said, winking. "You've got to get rid of the other guys. If you don't, then all bets are off."

Opening her eyes, Kat stared straight at Inez. "Kiss me."

Everybody was waiting for this moment. If Inez couldn't forgive her, then the future of the family would be endangered. Inez walked over to her lover, moving in seductively until their faces were close, their eyes meeting romantically. The women hugged, arms tightly around each other, and their mouths opened and there was a heated dance of tongues.

The last word came from the doctor, as she nodded approvingly. "Don't be frightened of change. Change is good. Growth is good. Every romantic relationship that comes into your life will leave a mark, sometimes a permanent one. Just don't move too fast."

All was right in the world. Kat, on the drive to the apartment, called all of her "outside" fellas and fired them. Alex was grinning ear-to-ear while Inez sat quietly, watching us with a mischievous smile. Everyone breathed a sigh of relief; the family was saved.

At the apartment, everyone stripped Kat and covered her with wet kisses and caresses. We let her know how valuable she was to the family, which would not exist without her. First, Alex made love to her tenderly like a shy junior high student caught in the throes of calf-love. Kat giggled. Then Inez had her turn, ignoring her face, instead surrounding her hard nipples with her tongue. Her fingers played along the woman's soft, smooth body. Kat covered her eyes with her hands while her lover parted her thighs and focused on her pussy, placing a finger inside. She flicked her tongue lightly between her sex lips, sucking them gently, and then sucking her swollen clit. Kat's hands clutched her lover's face against her, grinding and bucking into the sensations generated by her mouth. The pleasure rose to the point where her arousal was off the charts, drowned out by the screams of need and desire. Inez continued to finger-fuck her until she could barely move, just whimper.

"I saved the best for last," Inez said, slapping my hand like a tag-team wrestler would. "Go, get 'em, Tiger."

"No more foreplay," Kat said, with a sweat-drenched face. "Just pound the pussy. Time for some hard-core fucking!"

I kneeled behind her, moving her moist legs farther apart.

She shuddered with the penetration of my thick dick stretching her, as she shoved her behind up more. With a gasp, I rammed it as far as it could go inside her, double-pumped, and pulled it back out with a pop. She was bouncing back against me, fucking me, my rod hitting something inside.

"Don't stop . . . please," she murmured. I was crazed.

By that time, her shouts had brought everybody back out and they sat, watching us perform. Somehow this was different. For some reason, this was so much better than I remembered, so weird, so intense, so feverish. Kat belonged here. We belonged with Kat here. We were family. We loved each other.

ONE LAST FLING

Kristina Wright

"We're Vegas bound," Douglas said, helping me into the back of our limousine.

The neon lights of Club Europa reflected off my silver-sequined minidress, making me sparkle like a disco ball. I made a halfhearted effort to preserve my modesty as I climbed in, tugging my skirt with one hand while I held a glass of champagne in the other. I wasn't particularly successful at either, as I felt a cool breeze on my ass and the trickle of champagne on my wrist.

I fell into the back of the limo in a fit of giggles and waited for my entourage to join me. "Oh, but I'm not finished dancing!"

Alex got in beside me, his long limbs tangling with mine as we made room for two more. "It's three hours to Vegas and the girls are waiting for you. You'll dance the night away tomorrow night."

"Fuck the night away, is more like it," Douglas said, as he and Neil climbed in and sat across from us.

Neil tapped the partition between the driver and us. "We're ready," he called. "Let's get the bride to Vegas."

The limo pulled away from the curb in front of my favorite dance club and I waved good-bye as if I would never see it again. I was giddy and tipsy and very cozy in the back of the limo with my three favorite men—besides my fiancé, Simon, of course. Not that I don't have female friends; I do. They were waiting for me at the Bellagio in Vegas and in the morning we'd be getting massages and pedicures and talking about boys before I walked down the aisle. But I had wanted my last night as a single woman to be spent with my three closest guy friends.

It had been Simon's idea for my bachelorette party to end up in Vegas, where we were to be married the following evening. Now, I was floating happily along thanks to the beautiful, bubbly champagne that kept flowing into my glass from endless bottles provided by my attentive staff of three. I was dressed in sparkly sequins and smoky mascara, looking very much the party girl out for a night of dancing and debauchery. I smiled like the proverbial cat that has eaten the cream and curled up contentedly on the leather seat next to Alex.

"Well, lady, did we show you a good last night?" Alex asked, refilling my glass yet again.

I sighed as I sipped the expensive champagne. "Absolutely. We made quite a scene."

It was true. We'd popped into three clubs over the course of the evening and caused a bit of a stir every time as I led the men out to the center of the dance floor. I loved having all eyes on me and my boys. Alex, at six-four and with almost white-blond hair attracted enough attention on his own. But throw in former football player Douglas, with his rugged good looks, and lean, muscular Neil with the body of a runner, and I knew every woman in every club was jealous of me. The best part was feeling safe, surrounded by men who knew me at least as well as Simon did. I snuggled against Alex's shoulder and sighed. Douglas and Neil sat across from us, drinking beer from the well-stocked limo fridge.

"I could get used to this, if I wasn't getting married tomorrow."

Douglas winked at me. "Why would you trade in wild nights of dancing with your own personal harem for boring married life?"

"Aren't harem boys usually eunuchs?"

"Definitely no eunuchs here," Alex said, gruffly.

We laughed at that. Alex's sexual conquests were almost as legendary as, well, my own. I'd tested those waters a time or two and decided he had earned his reputation as a cocksman. Of course, Douglas wasn't a slouch in the bedroom, either. The only mystery for me was Neil. Bedroom-eyed, soft-spoken Neil was a big question mark to me. I glanced at him now— wondering things probably better left unknown.

The limo turned a corner a little too sharply, which pressed me closer to Alex. "Hey, Mr. Limo Driver," I called through the darkened partition. "Take it easy. I'm getting married tomorrow."

The partition lowered enough for me to see blue eyes staring at me in the rearview mirror. "Yes, ma'am. My apologies."

I giggled. "S'okay."

"It's official," Neil said. "She's drunk."

I harrumphed in a very unladylike fashion. "I am not drunk. I'm just a little bit tipsy."

Alex's hand, which had been on my knee since the corner-turn, seemed to have accidentally slid up my thigh. "Well, I'm drunk."

He stroked my thigh seductively and his fingers felt warm on my bare skin. I couldn't tell if he was messing with me or being serious. The possibility that he might be serious was exciting— and also proof that I was most definitely a little drunk. I made a low murmur of pleasure and the three men laughed. I didn't like that at all. I was the bride, damn it. I wanted to be pampered and coddled and . . . other things.

"Uh-oh. Watch out, Alex," Douglas said. "You know how she gets when she's drunk."

I tilted my head and finished the last of the champagne in my glass before holding it out for another refill from Alex's bottomless bottle. "Do tell, Douglas. How *do* I get?"

"Oh, love, you know how you get," Alex answered good-naturedly as he poured. "Don't you?"

Alex, more so than the other two, always knew how to calm me down from one of my bitchy moods. I looked into his twinkling green eyes and smiled. I covered his hand with mine, wondering if I dared move it just a couple of inches higher. The thought made me squirm and sigh.

"Oh yeah. I remember now." I licked my lips, noting the way his gaze followed the tip of my tongue from one corner of my mouth to the other. " I get very *needy* when I'm drunk."

"Very needy," Alex said. "That's certainly one way of phrasing it, babe."

"She's *needed* me on more than one occasion." Douglas smirked, giving Neil's shoulder a nudge as if the whole thing was a big joke. "Haven't you, doll?"

I pouted. "I don't remember."

"I remember." Alex topped off my champagne glass. "Douglas's birthday, three years ago. You did naughty things with his birthday cake and then you disappeared into his bedroom for a good half hour—"

"It was an hour," Douglas interrupted.

"Fine, a good hour. And when you came out you had birthday cake in your hair—"

Douglas laughed. "Among other places."

"I did not!" Of course I had, but I felt like I needed to defend my feminine honor in face of their laughter at my exploits.

"Then there was that night we got thrown out of that club— what was the name of it?—because you pulled me into the bathroom. The *women's* bathroom," Alex went on.

I glared at him. "My zipper broke on my dress."

"Before or after he went into the bathroom with you?" Douglas asked.

Neil had remained quiet through their ribbing, but now he finished his beer and shook his head. "You've never *needed* me."

I opened my mouth to say something, but he was right. All of my drunk fooling around over the years had been with Alex and Douglas, mostly because I knew they didn't take it more seriously than what it was. Neil was different, though. I always suspected he had a bit of a thing for me and while I adored him and thought he was sexy as hell, my attraction to him was purely physical. I might play with the boys, but Simon had my heart and I felt like that was the one part of me Neil might demand if I let things go too far. But I couldn't help but wonder what I had missed.

"My loss." I gave Neil a sad smile. "You know I love you anyway, right?"

"I don't think we're talking about love here," Neil said, looking away as the limo moved through the quiet city streets.

The mood had shifted and I looked at Alex with dismay. Sensing my discomfort, he offered, "Well, the night's still young—and she's definitely drunk enough to be needy."

The men laughed, even Neil, and I relaxed a little. It was hard to think about Neil's hurt feelings with Alex's hand making slow, sensual circles on my thigh. I wriggled against him, which moved Alex's hand just a bit higher on my leg and under the edge of my skirt. He was so very close to touching my pussy I considered how much more I could slide down before I would be on the floor. It was a fleeting thought—and an unnecessary one. Alex spread his fingers on my thigh. His long fingers. Then he wiggled them lightly against the edge of my panties until I bit my lip to keep from moaning.

"Guess she's feeling needy," Neil said. "Is the bride-to-be wet already?"

I made a face at him. "That's rude."

"Yes, it is," Alex agreed. "And I don't know if she's wet."

They laughed at me again. I couldn't help but laugh with them as I enjoyed the feeling of Alex's finger rubbing lazily against me. "You are all so bad," I said. "And I love it."

Alex leaned down to whisper in my ear, "If you spread your legs just a bit, babe, I promise you will love it even more."

How can a girl say no to that? I did as he suggested, spreading my thighs far enough apart that my skirt rode up to my hips and gave Douglas and Neil a glimpse of my lacy white panties. I watched them watching me, getting more and more turned on by the way the night was going. Alex cupped my panty-clad pussy and gave it a gentle squeeze. I gasped, Douglas groaned, and Alex made an appreciative sound low in his throat. Neil just stared, his heavy-lidded eyes watching me. I looked past him and saw another pair of eyes staring at me from the rearview mirror. I smiled and winked, thoroughly enjoying the attention.

"Oh yes, the little minx is quite wet," Alex confirmed. "Despite your little white virginal panties, I think you're the bad one, Victoria."

I nodded in agreement. "Oh yes, I'm quite bad."

"Should I stop then?"

By way of an answer, I covered his hand again and pressed it to my pussy. "You'd better not."

"We're almost to the highway," the driver announced. "Shall I make one last rest stop before the drive to Las Vegas?"

Just then, Alex slipped a finger under the edge of my panties and pushed just the tip into my pussy. "Yes," I gasped. Then, quickly, "No, no! That won't be necessary."

"Excuse me, ma'am?"

I met the driver's eyes in the rearview mirror again, wondering just how much of our backseat antics he could see.

"I'm sorry, we were talking about something else," I said breathlessly as Alex pushed his finger inside me just a little bit farther.

Douglas and Neil exchanged amused looks.

"This is the best conversation I've ever had," Neil said, seeming to have recovered his sense of humor. I liked him better this way—my familiar old friend instead of the one who might have gotten away.

I stuck my tongue out at them. "Just drive, please."

"Certainly, ma'am," the driver said. "We should be in Las Vegas in a little under three hours. Let me know if you need anything."

"I wouldn't mind doing a little less talking," Douglas said. "I think actions speak louder than words."

I heard something in his voice that promised pleasure. For me. The combination of champagne and familiarity had left me utterly without inhibitions.

"What would you like to do, Douglas?" I asked, raising my hips to Alex's questing hand. Alex obliged me by sliding his hand down the front of my panties and giving my bare pussy a squeeze.

Douglas slipped to his knees on the floor of the limo. "I'd like to have my mouth too full to talk."

"Seems like she's already occupied," Neil commented. Whatever his feelings for me, he was clearly enjoying the show.

As if by silent agreement, Alex withdrew his hand from my panties and pulled the lacy fabric to the side. My bare, bikini-waxed—and increasingly wet—pussy was exposed to Douglas's view. He moved forward between my legs, pushing my knees apart with his hands. I squirmed on the seat, my pulse quickening in anticipation of what was to come. But Douglas made me wait. He stared at my exposed pussy, nostrils flaring as if he was taking in my scent. He was so close that I could feel the warmth of his breath on my aroused flesh. The silence in the limo was almost tangible—even the road sounds seem to have faded beneath the pounding of my heart.

"Lick her," Alex said, giving voice to my silent plea. "She's dying for it."

Douglas looked into my eyes, one eyebrow cocked, as if seeking my permission.

I nodded. "Please."

His tongue felt like velvet on my engorged sex. With the broad flat of his tongue, he lapped at me. I moaned, raising my hips to his mouth, wanting more. He licked me slowly, as if we were alone and had all the time in the world, his tongue dipping between the valley of my pussy lips and up over my swollen clit. Again and again, he licked me with those slow, methodical strokes designed to torment even while they gave me pleasure. I moved my hips against his mouth, seeking more.

Alex slipped the strap of my dress over my shoulder, exposing my breast. Then he dipped his head to suck my nipple into his mouth. I moaned, tugging the other strap down and cupping my breasts, offering them to Alex's lips. Douglas shifted lower, hooking my legs over his shoulders as he devoured me with his mouth.

I looked at Neil. He watched the three of us, his expression one of barely controlled lust as his hand moved slowly over the crotch. It excited me to know he was watching—an observer rather than a participant. I wanted more, though. I wanted to see him stroke himself. I opened my mouth to say just that, but Alex chose that moment to flick my clit with his finger as Douglas dipped his tongue between the lips of my pussy. I moaned, the combination of sensations driving me out of my mind and to the brink of orgasm. I tucked my head against Alex's shoulder, my eyes fluttering closed as I pushed my aroused body at the two men who pleasured me.

"She's going to come," Alex said.

Douglas's tongue licked along my wet opening while Alex stroked my clitoris with his fingertips. I clutched at Douglas's hair and tightened my thighs around his bent head. Every muscle in my body went taut, my damp skin feeling hypersensitive in my arousal. Then Douglas sucked my clit—and Alex's finger—into his mouth and I came.

"Oh, yes!" I gasped, nearly sliding off the seat as my orgasm slammed into me. "Oh god!"

"You naughty little girl. Come hard for us," Alex whispered in my ear. "Come on his tongue. Show us what a very bad girl you are."

I rode wave after wave of orgasm as Douglas nursed gently at my throbbing clit and Alex whispered dirty talk in my ear. When I gently nudged Douglas away from my sensitive clit, his mouth shiny with my wetness, he grinned and licked his lips.

"Delicious."

"Thanks," I said, feeling a little lightheaded.

Alex squeezed my pussy again. "So juicy. I don't think you're done."

I shook my head. "I don't think so, either."

Douglas moved my legs off his shoulders and shifted onto the bench seat beside me. Now, Alex and Douglas sat on either side of me while our silent observer sat across from us. If Neil felt left out of our debauchery, he didn't show it. He smiled, sipping his beer and looking from my face to my still-spread legs.

I took a steadying breath, my pulse still throbbing. "This is turning out to be quite a bachelorette party."

"If you were a guy, we would be at a strip club right now buying you lap dances from pretty girls pretending to get off," Alex said.

"Sexy boys stripping and getting off for me would be more fun, I think."

For the first time—perhaps ever—I think I shocked them. Alex and Douglas went very still on either side of me. Neil glanced out the tinted window at the darkness racing by. I laughed at their sudden incongruous modesty.

"C'mon, you have seen each other naked at the gym count-less times," I said. "What's the big deal about getting naked for me?"

There was a lot of throat clearing and looking anywhere but at me while I shook my head at how silly they were being. Men who thought nothing of revealing the naughtiest, kinkiest details of their sex lives, not to mention watching me expose myself and writhe in pleasure in front of them, were suddenly shy schoolboys when it came to stripping down in front of each other.

Alex was the first to break the awkward silence. "Naked and, er—*naked*—are two different things." He gestured toward his lap where his erection made an impressive tent. "I wouldn't want to intimidate these guys, after all."

"Yeah, right," Douglas snorted. "That's the reason I don't want to strip in front of you—I'm intimidated by your enormous dick."

"Mmm," I murmured, running one fingertip along the hard ridge of flesh in Alex's pants. "Enormous dick. I vaguely remember . . ."

Alex snorted. "Vaguely? I'd think it would be etched in your memory."

While the three of us were joking around, Neil watched and kept silent. I studied him as Alex and Douglas continued to trade barbs about the size of their equipment. Though his body appeared relaxed, with his legs stretched out in front of him and his arms across the back of the seat, he was staring at me hungrily. I liked the way he looked at me, as if I were the only thing that could satisfy him. It reminded me of Simon.

"You're awfully quiet," I said. "What do you think, Neil?"

He shrugged. "It's your party, babe. If you want me to get naked and jerk off, I'll get naked and jerk off."

Suddenly, I lost all interest in Alex and Douglas. They were familiar, predictable. Men's men. Or boys' boys. They'd goad each other into doing something neither of them would willingly do on his own. On the other hand, Neil—whom I had always assumed to be the more prudish of the three—was willing to do whatever I wanted without coaxing or bribery. I loved it.

"That would be . . . delicious," I said, searching for just the right word. "You'd do that for me?"

Neil nodded solemnly. "If that's what you want."

"I guess Neil is the only one who wants to make me happy," I teased.

Douglas and Alex were still quiet, sitting on either side of me like silent bodyguards. I could feel the tension in the confined space as they contemplated their options. Neither wanted to back down, especially when they thought they had the upper hand over Neil, who had missed out on the fun thus far. Their desire for whatever kinky games might transpire once they were naked was still outweighed by their heterosexual drive to be the only man in play.

Neil made the first move. If he was embarrassed to strip down while the three of us watched, he didn't show it. He only had eyes for me as he loosened his tie and unbuttoned the cuffs of his shirt. While there is a certain pleasure in watching a man undress, I found myself anxious for him to hurry. I had never seen him naked before. I had never even kissed him, much less touched his bare chest. Suddenly, I was sure the look in his eyes was mirrored in my own. Desire. *Need.* A strong physical pull. I wanted him. And since this was the only time I would ever have him, I wanted to take my time enjoying him.

Part of me felt guilty for ignoring Alex and Douglas as Neil stripped off his shirt to reveal a lean torso and finely sculpted muscles. These two men had been my friends and play partners in the past and there was no reason to exclude them now, even if my attention would be focused on Neil. Of course, it really depended on whether they would participate, but I fully intended to give them the chance.

"Well, boys, what about you?" I asked them, resting a hand over each of their crotches. Their arousal turned me on almost as much as Neil arching up off the seat to tug off his trousers.

"What about us?" Douglas asked, sounding almost offended even as his cock twitched beneath my gentle stroking.

"Neil isn't the only one who is going to get naked, is he?"

At that moment, Neil stripped off his confining boxer briefs, revealing a thick, heavily veined cock. He sat back down, his hand curling around his erection as he looked at me for instruction.

"That depends," Alex said, his voice thick with lust. "What's in it for us?"

I laughed. "Like the man said, it's my party, *babe*. You'll just have to get naked and find out."

Then there were two more men undressing in the limo as it headed for Las Vegas. I felt drunk on more than champagne as I watched them reveal themselves for my pleasure. I was dizzy trying to look from one to the other, watching as Douglas stripped off his shirt and exposed that muscular torso I had once rubbed against until I had a very wet orgasm. Then I was staring at Alex as he unfastened his pants, revealing the fabric of his underwear stretched tautly over his erection.

"I guess we know who the *bigger* man really is," Alex conceded, glancing at Neil. It was true—even without a measuring tape it looked as if Neil had a couple of inches on both of them. Not that it mattered to me, but I was excited to know they were looking at each other, too.

I stroked Alex's cock through his pants. "It's not the size of the ship—"

"It's the motion of the ocean," he finished with a grin. "I remember rocking the waves pretty hard a few times."

"Oh yeah," I breathed as he lowered his mouth over mine.

We kissed hungrily, tongues tasting of beer and champagne. I freed him of his pants and squeezed his cock until he moaned into my mouth. He returned the favor by fondling my breasts, tweaking my nipples hard just the way I liked.

"Hey, what about me?"

Eyes closed, I shifted to kiss Douglas. The taste and texture of him was different from Alex—rougher, more nipping of teeth than caressing of tongues. Alex continued to pinch and squeeze

my nipples as I used my other hand to play with Douglas's erection. A cock in each hand, my breasts being played with while I
kissed each in turn—I felt like my senses were being overloaded.

I couldn't find a rhythm because each man's attention was
different. Alex was slow and languid, Douglas was quick and
intense. I was caught between their desires, my own building
to an almost painful need. I crossed and uncrossed my legs, my
pussy sadly neglected.

I remembered Neil and pulled my mouth away from Douglas
to look at him. He was angled in the corner, one leg stretched
out along the seat, the other bent at the knee. He fisted his
heavy cock as he watched us, a thoughtful smirk on his face. I
wondered what he was thinking as he made long, slow strokes
up the length of his erection. I not only wanted his body, I
wanted inside his head.

"Let me know when you're ready for me," he said, when he
saw the direction of my gaze.

Those few words were enough to make me whimper in need.
I watched Neil while I continued to play with the two cocks on
either side of me. I mimicked his strokes, feeling some strange
pull toward him that I had never had—or never admitted to—
before. While Douglas and Alex made guttural sounds of pleasure, Neil remained silent, that enigmatic smile in place as he
showed me how he pleasured himself.

"I want you," I whispered. "*Now.*"

Everything changed between us with that proclamation.

Neil's smile was pure satisfaction, as if he had already gotten
the sexual release he craved. "Anything the lady wants."

"What about us?" Alex asked, closing his hand around mine
as I stroked him.

"I want Neil."

Douglas whispered hoarsely, "Just don't stop touching me."

Neil followed Douglas's lead from earlier, slipping to his knees in front of me. I spread my legs, offering myself like a gift. He dipped his head between my thighs and licked me—softer than Douglas, like he was licking foam from a latte. I sighed, shifting forward on the seat to give him full access. I was sure I was leaving a puddle on the limo upholstery, but I didn't care.

I spread my legs over Alex and Douglas's legs. Each of them put a hand high on my thigh, as if framing my pussy for Neil's pleasure. I met the bemused gaze of the driver in the rearview mirror and winked at him before closing my eyes and giving myself over to the pleasure of Neil's slow, infuriating licks. He nibbled my labia, sucking each plump lip into his mouth before circling my clit with the tip of his tongue. When I didn't think I could bear the teasing any longer, he took my swollen clit between his lips and sucked it.

I gasped, whimpering, "Oh, I can't take any more! It's too much!"

I reflexively tried to close my legs, but Alex and Douglas held me spread for Neil's enjoyment. I still held their cocks in my hands, squeezing and stroking them in rhythm to my own pleasure, aroused more than I'd ever been in my life.

Just as I felt the first tremors of orgasm low in my belly, Neil pulled away.

"No," I gasped. "Please!"

"I'm going to fuck you," he said simply. "But I don't have a condom."

"No problem, dude," Alex said, fumbling with his discarded trousers. "Here."

Neil took the proffered square with a grin. "Always prepared."

Alex inhaled sharply as I ran my thumb over the glistening

tip of his cock. "Yeah, but I thought I was the one who would be using it."

The rip of the condom packet made me moan. "Hurry," I said. "I need you."

"I need you, too," Neil said, and then he was inside me.

After feeling open and vulnerable, I was suddenly, almost impossibly, full. I took a deep, steadying breath as Neil slowly pushed inside my wetness. He stared into my eyes and the intimacy was too much. I tilted my head back against the seat and closed my eyes, whimpering when his cock was fully inside me.

"Look at me," he demanded. "Watch me fuck you."

The tone of his voice demanded immediate compliance. I jerked my head up, staring first into his hard, almost unfamiliar face, then looking down to where we were joined, his olive skin looking so much darker against my paleness.

"That is so fucking hot," Douglas said softly.

I looked at him and saw that he, too, was staring between my legs and watching Neil fuck me. A quick glance on the other side confirmed that Alex was equally mesmerized by the scene before him. My orgasm had subsided enough for me to regain something of my control and I began to slowly stroke the men on either side of me in time to Neil's strokes. I was fleetingly reminded of a horse and jockey, both moving in tandem, joined in a powerful race to the finish.

Neil gripped my ass, pulling me down hard on his cock even while Alex and Douglas still held my legs open. "So fucking tight," he growled.

I moaned, a pain-and-pleasure sensation cutting through me like a dangerously sharp knife. I kept my eyes on Neil, letting him see what he was doing to me. He fucked me in long, deep strokes, withdrawing his cock until the head was just inside my opening before slamming inside me again. Every motion brought a moan to my lips and a plea for more. My skin was damp with sweat and I felt dizzy from the heat of our bodies moving together.

"Come on my cock," he demanded. "I won't come until you do."

I felt as if a knot of tension unwound low in my belly. I undulated against him, rocking my hips for my own pleasure, squeezing and stroking Alex and Douglas as if they were extensions of my body. I felt wetness on my hands, but I didn't know if they had come or if it was sweat. I didn't care. They would tell me to stop when they were done, but none of us was ready for it to end. Not yet. Not quite yet.

Neil pulled back, thrusting shallowly just inside my pussy, the head of his cock stroking my sweet spot. I gasped, going tense and still. Then, suddenly, I was coming. Hard. My orgasm rocketed through me like an explosion, causing me to scream out my release. My body, still a moment earlier, went into motion, rocking on Neil's cock as if I would milk him dry.

Neil's answering groan as my pussy rippled around him was softer than mine, but the expression on his face told me the pleasure was no less intense. He flexed his hips one last time, his cock throbbing inside me. We stayed like that for a long moment, sweat-slick bodies joined together, until my orgasm subsided. Neil was still breathing hard as he pulled free of my body. I gasped, feeling suddenly bereft at his absence.

Alex cleared his throat. "You can release your death grip now," he said gruffly.

My giggle turned into a full-fledged laugh. In my excitement, I had been holding on to Douglas and him for dear life. Now I realized that both were going flaccid, having certainly enjoyed the moment.

"Sorry," I said.

Douglas stroked my thigh softly. "Don't be. It was pretty amazing until about five minutes ago when I started considering we might end up eunuchs after all."

I shifted on the seat, wincing at the stiffness in my thighs from being held open for so long. "Sorry, guys," I said.

I realized Neil hadn't spoken and I searched his face for what he might be thinking. That quiet smile was back in place—the one that was a little too serious to be amusement.

"You okay?" I asked as if we were alone in the limo.

He nodded. "Just grand."

"Thank you." There didn't seem to be much more to say. Except, "You are truly amazing."

"Back at you, babe," he said rakishly. "That was a dream come true."

The driver spoke up before I had time to contemplate the meaning of his words.

"We've arrived at the hotel, ma'am."

I looked out the window and saw the lights of the Bellagio sparkling like an oasis just outside the window. The night had passed and I would be getting married soon. Reality came rushing back like a splash of cold water in the face as I considered all the things I still needed to do. I was hardly in any position to get out at the moment, however.

I watched in drowsy detachment as the boys hurriedly dressed. Now that the party was over, they were anxious to beat a hasty retreat. I giggled. The champagne buzz had worn off, but the sex buzz was still going strong.

"Remember, what happened in the limo stays in the limo," I said conspiratorially.

"Right," Alex said. "Good to know."

Douglas grinned and shook his head at me as he tugged his trousers on. "Only you could get me to do that, lady."

I smiled. "I know."

"Aren't you going to get dressed?" Neil asked.

I nodded. "In a minute. I'll let you guys get out of here so I can straighten up in peace."

"I can wait for you," Neil said, still looking out for my needs.

The driver responded, "I'll make sure the lady gets to her room."

The guys exchanged looks, Alex raising an eyebrow at me. "Is that okay with you?"

"I'll be okay. Find the girls and tell them I'll be there in about an hour."

Douglas grinned, as if he knew something. "It looks like the lady's evening isn't finished, boys."

Alex and he laughed, but Neil just stared at me. "You've had too much champagne. I'm not leaving you alone with the limo driver."

I laughed. "It's okay, Neil." When he still didn't budge, I leaned forward and whispered in his ear. "Trust me. I'm safe with the driver."

Something in my tone made him turn around and look over the partition. He nodded. "I see."

Alex gave me a hug and a deep, soulful kiss before opening the limo door. "See you tomorrow, babe."

"Get some sleep," Douglas added, giving me an equally intense kiss. "It's going to be a busy day tomorrow."

Then they were gone and Neil was still watching me. "I don't know what to say."

I kissed his cheek. "Thanks for this memorable night. Truly."

He started to speak and I could see in his expression what he was going to say, so I kissed him. He hugged me as if he would never let go, but after a few moments he did. "See you tomorrow," he said before slipping out of the limo and closing the door behind him.

I waited until he had disappeared in the same direction Alex and Douglas had gone before saying, "Okay, you can come back here now."

The driver's door opened and closed and then the door closest to me opened and he settled beside me, his black hat at a jaunty angle. I tossed it on the seat across from us and mussed his wavy brown hair.

"Quite a night you had, Mrs. Rhodes," he said.

"I'm not Mrs. yet, Mr. Rhodes."

Simon angled me sideways onto his lap, brushing my hair from my damp cheeks. "Was it all you wanted it to be?"

I smiled, happy but also a little wistful. "And more. How about you?"

He chuckled. "Fantasy satisfied, though I wish I could have seen a bit more of *you*."

I stretched my arms out. "You can see me now."

His gaze roamed over my body. I was instantly conscious of what a picture I must present, with my dress bunched around my waist, my hair a tousled mess of blonde curls, my smoky mascara smudged beneath my eyes. I smiled.

"Like what you see?"

He nodded. "You look like one very satisfied woman."

I wiggled on his lap, feeling that urgency building again. "Almost. Not quite."

"You want *more*?" His mock surprise only made me laugh. "What an insatiable wench you are."

I slid to my knees and nudged his legs apart. He stared down at me as I unbuckled his belt and worked his zipper down over his heavy erection. I felt my pussy—still tender from earlier, but already wet—tighten in response to his arousal.

"Aren't you happy you're marrying me?"

He groaned as I freed his cock from his pants and gave the

tip a lick. "You are definitely a dream come true—*my* dream come true. Are you happy you're marrying me?"

I thought of Simon indulging my last fling with my three best friends while he fulfilled his fantasy of watching me. It didn't seem possible that two people could be more perfect for each other. I sighed in blissful abandon. Just before I gave Simon his last single-guy blow job, I looked up into his eyes and whispered, "Absolutely."

ABOUT THE AUTHORS

JANINE ASHBLESS has had many short stories published by Cleis, along with one novel: *Cover Him with Darkness,* a fantasy thriller (with lots of sex) about fallen angels and religious conspiracy. She lives in the North of England and has been in her current poly relationship for twelve years.

M. CHRISTIAN is a California-based writer who has extensively published in science fiction, fantasy, horror, thrillers, and even nonfiction. It is in erotica that Christian has become an acknowledged master with stories in anthologies including *Best American Erotica, Best Gay Erotica,* and too many other anthologies to name.

AMANDA EARL is Canadian writer and publisher, and managing editor of the Ottawa-based *Bywords.* She attempts to disturb the universe with art, poetry, music, photos, and occasional baked goods.

JEREMY EDWARDS is the author of some 150 erotic short stories and two novels, including *The Pleasure Dial: An Eroto-comedic Novel of Old Time Radio,* which won an Independent Publisher Book Award. His work has appeared in five volumes of *The Mammoth Book of Best New Erotica.*

ABIGAIL EKUE is an author, photographer, and provocateur. She's the author of the short-story collections, *The Darker Side of Lust* and *Exhaust Pipes.* Her art exists to stir thoughts and emotion.

REBECCA M. KYLE is a writer, editor, and cat herder who lives in the Southeastern US.

MAX LAGOS is a middle-aged, pansexual, polyamorous, kinky father of two, living in Toronto, Canada. Sex and sexuality are two of his favorite topics.

SOMMER MADSEN is a professional dirty-word writer, gluten-free baker, amateur runner, fat wiener dog-walker, and expert procrastinator. She lives in Baltimore, with The Bearded Goat, an eclectic collection of kids, and the previously mentioned fat wiener dog.

REMITTANCE GIRL is a Canadian writer, educated in Madrid and London. The writer spent fifteen years of her life in a small Southeast Asia country. Now in Spain, she writes stories about people and the strange ways in which their desires twist them into new beings.

TERESA NOELLE ROBERTS, a prolific author of short erotica, is also known for erotic romances—paranormal, kinky contemporary, and science fiction. She enjoys belly dance, yoga, cooking, hiking, and organic gardening.

THOMAS S. ROCHE is the author of numerous short stories, in the erotica genre, and occasionally dabbles in horror, crime, fantasy, and science fiction. His novel, *The Panama Laugh,* was a finalist for the Bram Stoker Award from the Horror Writers Association. His short story, "Butterfly's Kiss" was a finalist for the John Preston Award from the National Leather Association USA. He was the editor of *Eros Zine,* which won a Best of the Bay Award from the *San Francisco Bay Guardian.* He is currently pursuing his doctorate in clinical psychology with relationship counseling.

ANNE TOURNEY is a veteran writer of erotic short stories and novels since 1993. She enjoys exploring the ways that sexuality helps us transcend ordinary experience. She currently lives, writes, and reads in an off-the-grid home in rural Colorado.

KRISTINA WRIGHT is the editor of *Fairy Tale Lust* and a dozen other erotica anthologies of Cleis Press. Her short fiction has been anthologized in over 120 collections and her nonfiction has appeared in dozens of publications from *USA Today* to *Cosmopolitan.*

ABOUT
THE EDITOR

COLE RILEY is the pen name for a well-known journalist and reviewer. His work has appeared in several anthologies and magazines, including a recent stint as a columnist at *SexIs Magazine*. He has written several novels including *Little White Lies*, *Harlem Confidential*, *The Devil To Pay*, and *Guilty As Sin*. He has edited two popular anthologies: *Making The Hook-Up: Edgy Sex with Soul* and *Too Much Boogie: Erotic Remixes of the Dirty Blues*.